THE LEGEND OF MARA FLORES

ALSO BY ARTHUR MILLS

THE LEGEND OF MARA FLORES

ARTHUR MILLS

BRANCHING PLOT BOOKS

This book is for the women who learn systems because they have to survive inside them. The ones who read rooms, memorize routes, notice patterns, and fix problems before anyone admits they exist. The women who understand that power doesn't always sit at the top, and that the machine depends on those who know how to move through it without drawing attention.

It's for the women whose labor is treated as background noise. Who are expected to be reliable, calm, and invisible all at once. The women who carry responsibility without title, authority without recognition, and consequences without credit. The women who are trusted to hold everything steady, but never asked what it costs them to do so.

And it's for the women who endure anyway. Who keep things running because stopping would let everything collapse. You hold this place up. The machine knows and refuses to say so. Your name should be on it. This story puts a name to what the machine tries to keep nameless.

CHAPTER ONE

THE TOWER'S MORNING RITUAL

The Tower stood before dawn, a vertical grid of reflected sky and blank windows. Fifty stories tall and mirrored on every surface, it watched the city without blinking. Plaza lights pooled on the concrete, tinting everything blue: benches, poles, the wind kicked wrappers that skated in dry circles like they had nowhere better to be.

Inside, the lobby air was motionless but warm. The glass security desk sat on a chessboard of tile, sharp-edged and deliberately empty. A plastic orchid performed its permanent bloom. Light strips woke one at a time in a sequence programmed to suggest an invisible executive's path from door to elevator. The only movement was the brush of a cleaning crew's cart, wheels splaying silent lines across the polished floor.

***

In the basement, the Global Security Operations Center operated in a windowless bunker. The GSOC was a universe of blue screens, each one sectioned and timestamped, covering nearly every corridor and elevator.

The ceiling panels never flickered. Nothing inside aged. It was the closest thing the Tower had to a heartbeat, and even that was artificial, measured in pings, logs, and the soft click of a mouse.

The shift supervisor sat hunched at the central console, thumb scrolling through yesterday's incident log. Three false alarms. A delivery held at the loading dock. One flagged face at the staff entrance. Cleared. Logged anyway.

The operator on the B desk drank coffee from a stained ceramic mug. His shirt was company issue, but untucked, the hem catching against the rim of his chair. His face glowed white on the bank of monitors, each square a different angle: hallway, elevator, lobby, glass corridor, empty, empty, empty.

If you watched the feed in real time, there was almost nothing to see. Security footage was best consumed as background radiation, a flicker at the edge of your vision. Most nights, the B desk watched sports on their phones, volume low, closed-captioned. Pattern recognition was the actual job, the difference between a person who belonged and a person who might make things complicated.

***

Up on the plaza, the sky lit but didn't change. Clouds smeared the city's edges. Wind shoved at the Tower's glass face and got no reaction. Traffic lights cycled for no one, then blinked red for the first delivery van of the day.

At 5:28 a.m., Mara Flores stood at the staff entrance, right hand already reaching for her access badge, left hand tensing to push the door. She paused for the security lens, made eye contact with her own reflection, then held the access badge to the reader.

The reader blinked once, thinking.

It blinked again.

Mara didn't move. She waited. She could wait for machines. That was half her job.

Green. Lock release.

"Please step into the door," the automated voice said.

She stepped inside without slowing, but the second blink stayed with her. It had done that before, just yesterday.

The lobby's warmth met her like an old habit. The overhead strips triggered ahead of her, flicking on half a second before she passed beneath them. It was like walking in front of her own shadow, and after twenty years, the sensation still pleased her in a private, stubborn way. A small proof that she could still set something in motion.

No one spoke to her. No one needed to. The building registered her: motion sensors in the staff corridor, keypads, the internal clock on the espresso machine warming itself to readiness. It kept its attention on her the way it kept attention on everyone, quietly, completely, without affection.

Mara moved through the staff corridor with her jacket over one arm, shoes making soft echoes on tile. She hung her jacket in the shared locker and ran a hand down the front of her shirt, smoothing it into its morning shape. In the brushed steel of the elevator doors, she caught her own reflection: tired eyes, a controlled mouth. She adjusted her access badge until it sat flush.

The uniform was slate gray. The lanyard was white.

Temporary, the Tower called it. Every job here was technically contract, no matter how many years you had served. Mara had kept her access badge unscratched for two decades anyway. A record matched only by her consistency.

Her key ring was heavy with duplicates and relics. She fished the right one without looking, unlocked the side door, and stepped into the café's cool darkness. It smelled faintly of lemon oil and bleach, the only evidence that anyone cared for this place outside business hours. The espresso machine blinked a time that was always slightly wrong, two minutes behind the lobby's master clock.

Mara pressed the power button as if she were waking a sleeping animal.

The machine exhaled and clicked into its start-up cycle.

Lights over the counter came up in slow stages, pale bars across the pastry case. Mara moved through the small space with the efficiency of someone who didn't have to think about her hands.

Bins. Trays. Labels in marker that never quite scrubbed out.

She lined the baked goods up on the prep table, checked for cracks and flaws, and slid the shiniest turnovers to the front like she was dressing a window that would never get gratitude. She didn't waste judgment on things that never changed.

A reflection moved at the edge of the glass door.

Mara didn't startle. She flipped the lock.

Walt stepped in, shaking off imaginary rain from a morning that was bone dry. His security jacket had neon trim that looked bright even in the café's dim light. He was a year from retirement and carried it on his shoulders like something heavy and welcome.

"Morning, Flores," he said, drawing out the syllables just enough to be friendly.

"Morning," Mara replied, already filling the first water jug for the coffee tanks.

Walt leaned on the counter and watched her work the way people watched a familiar show. He didn't ask questions that mattered. He didn't expect answers that would change anything.

"Anything weird overnight?" he asked, because that was the ritual line.

Mara slid a tray of pastries toward the case. "Someone jammed a muffin into the HVAC vent again."

Walt grinned, pleased. "Kids these days."

He reached into his pocket and pulled out cash, always. He set two crumpled bills in the tip jar like he was making a small offering to keep the day from biting.

Then he hesitated, the first real hesitation Mara had seen from him in weeks.

"They did that thing again at the door," he said.

Mara didn't look up. "What thing?"

Walt scratched the side of his jaw. "That pause. Like the reader is deciding whether it knows you."

Mara kept her hands moving. Water jug. Lid. Counter wipe. If she stopped, the thought would take up more space than it deserved.

"It opened," she said.

"It always opens," Walt said, and his voice dropped without him meaning to. "That's what makes it weird. They told us not to worry about it."

Mara's fingers tightened around the edge of the counter until her knuckles lightened, then loosened again. She watched the espresso machine's display count upward as if numbers could anchor her.

Walt cleared his throat, replaced the mask of easy familiarity.

He took his coffee. He nodded once. He left.

***

At 5:50 a.m., the cleaners came through. Two women in identical blue polos, hair pulled into tight buns. Mara knew one as Lidia. The other was still the New One, even though six months had passed, and she still didn't speak.

They moved as a unit, wiping tables, replacing bins, straightening chairs to perfect angles. Mara made espresso for them without being asked.

"Gracias," Lidia said, sliding a cardboard sleeve over the cup. Her eyes were red from lack of sleep.

Mara nodded. There was an unspoken pact between early shift workers: get through the hours, take what you can from the day.

At 6:00 a.m., Mara rolled up the café gate. It clattered, loud in the otherwise silent lobby. The Tower was still half asleep.

The early arrivals came in a trickle. Maintenance clocked in through the loading dock and vanished below ground. Cleaning staff clustered in the lobby before dispersing like dye in water. HR arrived in a suit sharp enough to look structural. A young man in IT jogged across the marble without looking up from his phone.

The hierarchy announced itself in lanyards: color, width, the presence or absence of plastic card holders. The Tower couldn't resist a visible system.

Mara watched it from behind the counter with the calm of someone who understood the rules and had decided, long ago, not to play.

Marcy burst in late, out of breath, hair still damp from the shower, uniform worn in open violation. Sleeves rolled. Buttons undone. Pens behind each ear like earrings.

"Sorry, sorry, train," she said, as if the word could pay for her lateness, and then she was already grabbing the grinder, refilling it from the bulk bin. "Also. They tagged you again."

Mara slid cups into a neat row. "Who did?"

Marcy jerked her chin toward the ceiling, ignoring the cameras buried in walls. "GSOC. Staff entrance. Same thing. Your badge lagged, and the screen did that little box around your face."

Mara didn't look up. Looking made things feel real, and she didn't have room for that before the rush.

"It cleared," she said.

"Yeah," Marcy said, tamping espresso with unnecessary force. "It always clears. That's what is creepy. Like it wants to argue first."

Orders began to print. Espresso hissed. The bakery case gleamed under fluorescent bars. The Tower woke the way it always did. All at once.

***

At 6:40 a.m., the line hit the first crest. The regulars. Mara scanned faces, remembering each by their coffee preference and their gait. Some stayed, hoping for recognition, a smile. Others barked their orders and stared at their phones, already halfway into another life.

By 7:22 a.m., the rush hit full velocity. The line to the counter snaked past the velvet rope, each person lined with precise, half irritated spacing. It was always the same: sleep starved financial analysts, pale interns clutching notebooks, HR in monochrome heels, operations in brown leather loafers. The uniform code was invisible but absolute. You could guess a person's title by their shoes, the color of their lanyard, and how they held their phone, cradled or weaponized.

Mara worked the register while Marcy ran point on the espresso machine, their choreography so seamless it bordered on telepathy. Mara took orders, keyed them in, pivoted to assemble pastry bags, then pivoted back, never letting her face change.

A man in a pale lavender shirt ordered a triple red eye and acted like it was normal.

"Name for the cup?" Mara asked, though she already knew it.

"Clive," he said, and spelled it out even though it was five letters.

Mara wrote it cleanly. "Coming up, Clive."

The day's cadence was predictable in its cruelty. The more urgent the emails, the longer the line. The worse the sleep, the more complicated the orders. Most days, the challenge was caring just enough to get it right, and not enough to take any of it home.

A woman from Legal ordered two lattes, a cold brew, and a vegan cookie, all for delivery to a glass conference room. No eye contact. No pause in her typing. Her lanyard was platinum, a subtle flex she didn't have to announce.

Mara clipped the order to a tray and pushed it down the line with the efficiency of someone who had done this thousands of times.

Janis Miller, the janitor with a patient face and tired eyes, swept the lobby at a measured pace. She paused at the edge of the line, gave Mara a nod, and waited for the crowd to thin.

Sammy, maintenance, passed by with a stepladder slung over one shoulder and a toolbox in the other. He was in a mid-conversation with someone on his headset, but he made eye contact with Marcy and gave a two-finger salute before disappearing into the service hallway.

Marcy leaned in, voice lower. "Sammy's got a girlfriend, I'm telling you."

"Or a plumbing emergency," Mara said.

"Could be both."

A temp from HR came up holding her phone out like a shield. "Do you have almond milk that isn't sweetened?" she asked, making it a challenge.

"Yes," Mara said, then waited.

The woman narrowed her eyes. "Are you sure?"

"I'm sure."

She nodded once, decided Mara was telling the truth, and placed her order with a sigh. "This place," she said, not looking up. "It's like everyone's always watching."

Mara didn't smile. "They are."

The woman laughed as if it were a joke and walked away with her latte, as if the truth could be carried safely in a cup.

***

By 8:12 a.m., the rush collapsed. The line shrank to a trickle of late-comers, stragglers, and the odd visitor who didn't know the system and looked stunned by how fast the Tower demanded competence. Mara wiped the counter in slow, deliberate arcs, letting her muscles unclench.

Marcy exhaled a long, theatrical sigh and leaned against the machine.

"Every morning," Marcy said, "I think maybe today will be the day someone just brings us coffee."

"They would mess it up," Mara said, reaching for fresh sleeves. "Guaranteed."

Marcy grinned, then her eyes flicked past Mara's shoulder. "Walt's back," she said, rolling her eyes.

Mara didn't turn right away. She finished the stack. She aligned the sleeves. She gave herself one more second of routine before she let herself look.

Walt stood near the café gate instead of inside it. He was not buying coffee. His hands were empty. His shoulders were set in the posture of a man trying not to deliver a message.

He lifted two fingers, the small signal he used when he didn't want to be overheard.

Mara stepped to the edge of the counter.

Walt's mouth barely moved. "GSOC asked for you by name."

Mara held his eyes. "For what?"

Walt swallowed. "They said it's nothing. They always say that. But they told me to let you know, in case anyone asks."

"In case who asks?" Mara said.

Walt's gaze flicked to the lobby, to the glass desk, to the cameras that weren't visible unless you trained yourself to see them.

"Anybody," he said.

Mara nodded once. That was all she could afford. She turned back to the counter and picked up a rag that was already in her hand.

She wiped the same clean steel twice, slow and careful, until her breathing sounded normal again.

Behind her, the Tower kept moving. Lanyards swayed. Elevators opened and closed. The lobby caught its breath and let it out again.

Mara kept wiping anyway, because rituals mattered. If you stopped doing them, the day got loose at the edges.

And tomorrow, she had to wake up at 4:37 a.m. to do it all over again.

CHAPTER TWO

CRACKS IN THE ROUTINE

The next morning, at 4:37 a.m., Mara's alarm vibrated on the nightstand. A persistent pulse worked its way into her sleep and pulled her up in pieces.

Her first sensation was cold.

The heat in her one-bedroom apartment ran on a timer and hadn't kicked in yet. At some point in the night, she had kicked the blanket off, and now the air lay on her skin like damp plastic. She silenced the phone with one tired slap and lay still, letting the room come into focus.

The clock ticked in low increments, each second a blunt tap.

Mara took inventory the way she always did.

Left knee. Right shoulder. The tight pressure behind her eyes that promised a migraine by noon.

She counted to ten, like counting could redistribute fatigue, then sat up. The mattress squeaked, rubbery and familiar. She stayed on the edge long enough for the room to stop tilting.

In the kitchen, the envelopes waited where she had left them.

Bills, all of them. Some unopened. Some opened and folded back into their own threats. The top one was from Property Management Services, bold letterhead, the kind that always arrived with urgency and never arrived with mercy.

Mara ran a finger over the address window, felt the plastic give under her nail, and left it there.

Later, she told herself. After the shift.

She had been telling herself that for months.

The bathroom light was too bright. The mirror offered a version of her that looked slightly wrong, hair angled up in a tight bend, skin pale enough to read as blue under fluorescent light. She ran the faucet until the water stopped looking rusty, then drank from her hands, breathing through her nose to keep the chill from her teeth.

The shower ran hot, but weak. Mara stood under it with her eyes closed until the sting settled into something tolerable. She washed in the same order she always did. The routine kept her upright when the day didn't. Six minutes if she had to. Some mornings, that was the only kind of control she could afford.

She dressed without thinking. Uniform pants. The softer of her two shirts. Socks without holes. Hair into a low bun. Elastic tight enough to hurt.

Then she checked her access badge.

Still pinned. Still legible. Still temporary.

She held her gaze in the mirror for a second, then looked away.

The kitchen was barely a kitchen, more a corner carved out of the room. The table was just big enough for one person, though Mara rarely sat. She started the kettle, scooped grounds into the French press, and lined up her one mug like a tool.

The first swallow of black coffee was bitter and astringent, but it anchored her.

The envelopes sat inches from her hand.

She rinsed the mug, set it back on the rack, and checked her bag by habit: phone, wallet, keys. In the hall mirror, she wiped a faint smear off her cheek and forced her shoulders back into the shape that didn't invite questions.

She locked her door, then checked it again.

Down the hall, the vending machine buzzed in the dark like it had no business having power. Mara took the stairs two at a time.

Outside, the city was still asleep, or pretending to be. A distant garbage truck. A 24-hour pharmacy across the street, its sign buzzing. Streetlights cycling for no one. Mara kept her head down and walked fast enough to stay warm. She cut through a parking lot to steal twenty seconds, because twenty seconds was something she could still take without anyone noticing.

The Tower loomed ahead, a blunt rectangle of steel and glass, unchanged from yesterday, unchanged from the day before that. It always looked like it had been built to outlast the people inside it.

At the staff entrance, she had her access badge ready.

The reader blinked green. The lock released.

No pause.

That should have been relief. Instead, it felt like the building had decided not to argue today.

She stepped inside, and the lobby's warmth met her like an old habit. The building didn't welcome people. It processed them.

By the time she reached the café, the espresso machine was already warming its element, a low mechanical hum that felt like the start of the day whether she wanted it or not. The gate was still down, but a small cluster of regulars had gathered on the other side, faces lit by the cold glow of their phones. They stood in the loose formation of need and impatience, like they had been summoned by the smell alone.

Mara looked at the stenciled policy about on-time openings and pulled the gate up a minute early anyway. Rules mattered until they got in the way of keeping the day from spilling over.

Marcy was already on shift, sleeves rolled, pouring cold brew concentrate into a pitcher with the loose accuracy of someone pouring gasoline into a funnel. She looked up and grinned, eyebrows raised.

"It's like they camp out," Marcy said, shoving the pitcher into the fridge. "What do they think is going to happen, that we run out of coffee?"

"We might," Mara said.

The edges of the croissants blurred and re-formed when she blinked.

Marcy's grin shifted, the way it did when her brain ran a quick risk assessment. "You good?"

"Just tired."

Marcy accepted the way she accepted most things: with a calculation, then a choice not to press the live wire. She checked the hopper and said, "I had a dream I was trapped in here, and the only way out was through the pastry case. Like I had to eat my way to the street."

"You survive?"

"Woke up before I got to the muffins." Marcy gave the pastries a flat stare. "Symbolic."

The first customer ordered a triple shot and hovered at the end of the bar, eyes darting between his phone and whatever invisible countdown was ticking in his head. He wore an earpiece and talked to himself, punctuating with a click of his tongue.

Mara keyed the order and misfired once, wrong size. She erased it, corrected it, and handed the cup off without looking up.

The lobby filled the way it always did, in spasms.

Legal arrived in clusters, already talking like they were still in a meeting. IT drifted in half awake and sharp-edged. Two men in matching navy suits ordered in unison, as if it were a game.

Marcy ran the counter with chatter and jokes, as usual. Mara kept her answers short, as usual. The grinder's noise dulled her senses. The pressure behind her right eye tightened until it felt like a thumb pressing in. Every so often, her gaze flicked up to catch her reflection in the glass or the dark corner where a camera sat.

The thought tightened her shoulders. She forced them down and kept working.

A man with a black lanyard ordered five drinks for "a meeting." His access badge read Executive Services. He didn't bother with eye contact.

"Big meeting?" Marcy asked, lining up cups.

"Alignment session," he said. "I'm just the runner."

"You should unionize," Marcy said, and didn't bother to soften it into a joke.

The man grunted and moved to the pickup zone.

Mara scrawled names. Her hand shook. She paused, gripped the counter until the tremor passed, then kept going as if nothing had happened. When she looked up, Marcy was watching, just for a second, the way you watched someone carry a stack of plates that was one wobble away from disaster.

"You want me to take the register for a while?" Marcy asked, voice lower.

"I'm fine."

Marcy didn't argue. She just shifted her weight and stayed close enough to catch a fall without making it obvious.

The next rush came louder and messier. The register paper jammed. Marcy swapped the roll with quick, practiced hands.

Mara missed a step in the drink sequence and started a shot before the cup was ready. Espresso overflowed and scalded her thumb.

She jerked back, cursed under her breath, then wiped her hand on her apron and went back to work. The pain was sharp, then numb, the way the body decided some things weren't worth feeling yet.

By the time the lobby hit its meanest pitch, Mara's shirt clung damp to her back, and the noise swelled into a constant pressure, bouncing off marble and glass. Somewhere, a phone rang in an endless loop. Someone complained about the wait. Marcy shot back something sharp about premium demand. Mara didn't hear the exact words, just the rhythm of a fight that had happened a thousand times.

Sammy showed up with a toolbox in one hand and a thermos in the other, hair still wet from his morning shower. He set the thermos down and waited, calm as if the world couldn't touch him.

"What's broken today, Sammy?" Marcy called.

"Same as always." He cracked a small smile. "The universe."

Marcy laughed and poured him a drip coffee, black. "You want a Danish?"

"Not after last time." He lifted the thermos. "Thanks."

He slid a folded slip of paper across the counter to Mara. "You've got another leak," he said, voice neutral.

Mara unfolded it, scanned the highlighted line. "Where?"

"Back side of the cooler. Not urgent."

"Do we get hazard pay for mold exposure?" Marcy asked.

"Only if you grow an extra limb," Sammy said, and raised his cup in a two-finger salute before moving on.

When he was gone, Marcy leaned closer. "You ever notice he only shows up when you're on shift?"

Mara wiped the steam wand and pretended not to hear.

A new wave cut the conversation off. Mara reset her focus and repeated the sequence in her head like a mantra: cup, shot, pour, handoff, repeat.

Eventually, the line thinned. Manageable now. Marcy took the register and let Mara step back to restock. Mara moved through the motions, counting lids, checking inventory, making tiny repairs that would never get budgeted.

In the lull, Marcy wiped her hands and leaned in. "If I ever get out of here," she said, "I'm going to start my own place. No executives. No uniforms. No color-coded lanyards. No loyalty cards. Just coffee and honesty."

Mara glanced up. "Would you hire me?"

"Oh, no," Marcy said, grinning. "You'd run the place by lunch. I'd be out of a job."

They both smiled, real for a moment.

Then a man in a gray suit appeared at the counter with his phone held in front of his face. "I ordered a cold brew. Is it ready?" He didn't lower the phone.

Mara checked the bar. No cold brew. She scanned the tickets.

The order wasn't there.

A small, quiet drop hit her stomach. A moment where reality refused to align with what she knew.

"Sorry," she said. "I don't have it here. What's the name?"

He repeated it, then spelled it slowly, impatiently, blaming her for a system that ate orders.

Marcy glanced at the register. "It didn't go through. Can you just say it again?"

The man exhaled, repeated the order, then rolled his eyes up toward the ceiling as if the Tower itself had personally insulted him.

Mara made the drink, added ice, capped it, and handed it over with a practiced apology. He snatched it and walked away.

Marcy bumped Mara's shoulder, conspiratorially. "Not our fault."

The café went quiet again, thinly populated by a pair of interns in the corner, their laptops out, faces blank with ambition and exhaustion. Mara leaned against the bar for a few seconds and let the ache in her back settle.

When she caught her reflection in the glass, she didn't recognize herself for a second. Same face, wrong feeling. Like a copy that had been printed too many times.

She blinked and moved to the service nook for her break.

The nook was smaller than a janitor's closet: a sliver of counter, a battered chair, a supply cabinet, a fluorescent bulb that flickered once before settling into a steady pulse. Mara lowered herself into the chair and let her head rest against cool drywall.

For a minute, she did nothing.

Then she opened her bank app.

The interface was pale blue, designed to soothe. The numbers weren't soothing.

$41.67.

She scrolled down and saw the pending debits lined up like teeth: cell phone, insurance, utilities. After those hit, she would be in the red again. Deep red.

A notification popped up: rent due today.

She swiped it away.

She checked her email. The top message was from Property Management Services, flagged urgent. She didn't open it. She opened a spam offer instead, read three lines about a miracle vitamin, and deleted it. A small act of control, pointless and still necessary.

Another notification blinked. Important Information Regarding Your Tenancy.

Mara deleted it without reading.

The relief was immediate, physical, like loosening a belt that had been cutting into her ribs.

Tomorrow, she told herself. Maybe payday. Maybe next month.

Her break timer ticked down.

Mara checked her hair in the tiny mirror above the sink, pressed down strays, and straightened her access badge. She practiced the neutral face again. Then she stood and stepped back out.

The café had returned to its regular volume. The next wave was already beginning.

***

Closing took longer than it needed to. Mara wiped down the counter, ran bleach over every surface, and restocked pastries for tomorrow. Marcy counted the till and read numbers aloud as if she were narrating for an invisible audience.

"Short by six cents," Marcy said. "No one's going to miss it." She snapped the binder shut and glanced at Mara. "You ever notice the more you count, the less you care?"

"That's just practice," Mara said, scrubbing a dried milk ring off the espresso machine.

"I think it's survival," Marcy said, quieter now. "If I get promoted, will you cover my shifts?"

"They'd just give you more shifts," Mara said.

Marcy spun a pen between her fingers, staring at the floor. "Maybe I'll fake my own death. Start over somewhere with no coffee, no clocks, and, definitely, no cameras."

Mara liked the sound of that. She didn't say so.

They rolled down the café gate sharply at 2:00 p.m. Metal clattered through the empty lobby. Outside, the Tower's glass reflected city lights as if it were collecting them.

Marcy shouldered her bag and paused. "You heading out?"

Mara nodded.

"Walk with me to the bus?"

They left through the staff corridor, footsteps bouncing off cinderblock. At the exit, Marcy offered Mara a piece of gum as if it were a peace treaty.

Mara shook her head.

"It's the only vice I can afford," Marcy said, and peeled one for herself.

Outside, frost edged the empty flowerpots. Marcy blew a bubble, let it snap, then glanced sideways at Mara.

"You ever think about quitting. Just ever, I mean."

"Sometimes," Mara said, surprising herself with the honesty.

Marcy looked genuinely startled. "What would you do?"

Mara shrugged. "Probably this, somewhere else."

Marcy nodded, as if it made perfect sense. "You're too good at it. That's the problem."

They walked in silence for half a block. At the intersection, Marcy stopped. "This is me. If you ever want to talk about quitting, let me know." She grinned, all teeth, then jogged across the street toward the bus stop.

Mara watched her go, then turned for home.

Her route didn't change. Past shuttered storefronts. Past dead street-lights. Past the places the city pretended were temporary.

At her building, the hall smelled of bleach and something sweet, maybe a neighbor's perfume. Mara took the stairs two at a time to the fourth floor.

Outside her door, a new envelope waited, larger and thicker than the others, printed in red.

FINAL NOTICE.

It leaned against the door frame upright, accusatory, like it had taken the effort to stand.

Mara reached for it, then stopped.

Her hand hovered. She looked down the hallway. No one watching. No one to judge. No one to help.

She tucked the envelope under her arm, unlocked her door, and went inside.

The apartment was exactly as she had left it: cold, silent, the table still bare except for the morning's mug. She placed the envelope on the counter with the others and didn't open it.

She peeled off her jacket, hung it by the door, and sat at the table with her hands folded in her lap.

She listened to the pipes in the wall, the distant mumble of someone else's television. She stared at the red lettering until it blurred, then looked away.

Tomorrow, she told herself.

She would open it tomorrow.

CHAPTER THREE

THE LOCKOUT

Mara left the envelope unopened again and arrived at the Tower before the lights. She always did. The city was still ash on black, the lobby café locked behind its grate, and only the janitorial staff moved through the echoing tile. Mara keyed in at the service door and went through her opening steps: jacket off, hair pinned, hands scrubbed raw and dry from sanitizer. This morning, it was numbness layered over ache, like her body had come in early and left her behind.

At the staff entrance, a new sign had been taped up overnight, corners curling: **ACCESS BADGE REQUIRED. DO NOT HOLD DOORS.** Someone had written OKAY in marker under it. Someone else had crossed it out.

The air inside the café felt colder than usual. Maybe it was the way the HVAC cycled during off-hours, or maybe the weather had finally caught up with the building's glass skin. Mara hunched deeper into her shirt, shook the damp from her cuffs. She filled the espresso machine's tank, checked the pressure, and swept out the pastry case. Everything was ready, but her hands were slow. Even the machine's familiar clicks and sputters sounded muffled, as if wrapped in batting.

Marcy arrived at 5:50 a.m., voice bright enough to bounce off the glass. "Early crowd's already pacing out there," she said, rolling her eyes toward the silhouettes at the lobby entrance. "You'd think their stock portfolios would make them sleep in." She flicked her access badge at the lock, then ducked behind the counter, already in fast-forward.

Marcy's uniform was, as always, interpretive: shirt half-tucked, band logo visible through the thin gray fabric, two earrings in one lobe, and a chunk of blue nail polish missing from her right thumb. "You want me to run the bar today?" she asked.

"I'll start the register," Mara said. The words came out low, hoarse.

Marcy noticed. She always did. "Rough night?"

"Just didn't sleep."

Marcy nodded, nothing more required, and set to loading the first batch of beans. The smell was immediate, strong, oily, almost burnt. Mara preferred it that way. It cut through the haze.

They opened the gate at 6:00 a.m. The regulars trickled in, faces scrubbed, hair slicked to workday angles. Mara moved through her paces, taking orders and scanning access badges, her mind floating two seconds behind her body.

The banter helped. Mara found herself settling into the rhythm of the morning: three orders, then a pause; two lattes, then the spit of a receipt. It was all muscle memory.

At 6:37 a.m., a pair of construction men hit the counter, boots caked in road salt. One of them squinted at the tip jar, then jerked his chin at Mara. "You see the rent signs on Oak? Five hundred jump in one year. Landlords out here think we're made of money."

Marcy grinned. "I wish. My landlord thinks I'm running an unlicensed animal rescue."

"What kind of animals?" the second guy said, grinning into his phone.

"Mostly mice, some spiders. But I don't discriminate."

They all laughed. Mara did, too. The word rent pinged in her head and kept bouncing until it landed on the envelope sitting on her counter at home: **FINAL NOTICE**, bold and impassive. She hadn't opened it. She didn't need to.

The lobby filled in increments, the line thickening at the turn of every half hour. Mara lost herself in the repetition: take the order, ring it in, swipe the card, hand off the cup. She liked the certainty of steps, the clarity of transaction. But the sense of being off persisted, like static under the day's soundtrack.

At 7:16 a.m., the café's second register jammed. Mara tugged the drawer once, then set her thumb against the track and pressed until the plastic gave with a small click. A crumpled slip of paper came loose. She smoothed it, fed it back through the slot, and rang a test sale. The drawer slid open clean.

Good enough.

Marcy watched her do it. "How do you always know where to press?"

Mara wiped her thumb on her apron. "It catches in the same spot every time."

Marcy made a face like she wanted to ask more, then didn't. She grabbed the bleach spray and went back to wiping down the bar.

By 8:00 a.m., the rush was over. The lobby emptied out, leaving only the scent of aftershave and scorched bagels. For a moment, Mara considered checking her bank app, the way you might check a wound to see if it had stopped bleeding. She pulled out her phone, woke the screen, then locked it again without looking at the notifications.

She already knew what she'd see.

The rest of the day came in smaller waves and long stretches of routine. Mara moved through them by muscle memory, letting the predictable work keep her upright. When closing finally came, the predictability helped. Mara wiped down the espresso machine, emptied the bins, and restocked what little was left. Marcy did her part, then clocked out, tapping Mara's shoulder with a damp sleeve on her way past.

"See you, Flores," she said, and the door banged softly behind her.

Mara waited sixty seconds, then keyed out of the café. The staff corridor was hollow, the lights timed to flick on ahead of her. She left through the loading dock exit on the far side of the building, the air outside biting at her face and fingers. She zipped her thin old jacket and kept walking, shoes making no sound on the wet concrete.

The streets were mostly empty. Delivery vans idled at the curb, hazard lights blinking. Across the avenue, the pharmacy's neon flickered: OPEN 24/7, but the windows showed only shelves and shadows.

She took the long way around the block, stopping at the bank's glass hallway, where the ATM glowed. There was a man already inside, hands deep in the pockets of his expensive suit jacket. He punched the screen with slow, deliberate presses, then pulled a stack of bills and fanned them, counting each one in the light.

Mara waited, eyes fixed on her reflection in the door. She looked tired. The makeup she'd put on at five was gone, erased by steam and sweat. Her hair had come loose in the back, strands escaping the tie. She ran a finger along the edge of her jaw, then dropped her hand.

The man left, bills folded tight. He nodded at her without meeting her eyes.

Mara stepped in, slid her card into the slot, and typed her PIN.

The screen read: AVAILABLE BALANCE: $13.91.

She checked again. Same result.

Her stomach flipped, but the feeling was dull, like remembering a pain that had already faded. She printed the mini statement, tore it off, and slipped it into her pocket. The paper was thin and slightly damp, the ink already smearing.

Outside, the sky was turning gray. She walked toward her apartment, counting steps out of habit. At the crosswalk, she hesitated, then turned left, past the closed pizzeria and the darkened laundromat.

Scenarios ran on a loop in her head: call the property office, explain about the bank delay, ask for an extension, promise to pay in a week. Maybe two. Maybe beg, if it came to that. She could sell the TV, take on more shifts, figure it out tomorrow.

Her building's front door was propped open with a plastic bin. Mara saw it from the end of the block and knew, before she let herself know.

She slowed. A blue panel truck was double-parked at the curb, engine ticking. The logo on the side read: RHINO DISPOSAL: WE MAKE ROOM. Someone had dragged a dirty thumb through the word ROOM.

She told herself she could still turn around.

Her feet kept going.

In the lobby, the air smelled like wet cardboard and old bleach. She climbed the stairs two at a time, shoes sticking to the wax. On her floor, the hallway was full of strangers. Three men in matching T-shirts moved past her in a tight formation, her futon tipped on its side between them. One corner dragged against the wall, leaving a dark scrape.

At her landing, the property manager waited with a clipboard and a set of keys. He looked past her first, down the stairs, then finally at her face. He didn't look surprised.

"Ms. Flores," he said. "You're not supposed to be here right now."

Mara reached for the railing. "It's my apartment."

"Not as of this morning." His voice stayed even. "You got the notices. I know. They're right there on your counter."

She thought of the stack on the counter, the red letters she'd moved from one side of the sink to the other instead of opening. "I thought I had another week."

"That isn't what it says here." He tilted the clipboard toward her. The paper shook a little in his hand. "Signed by the sheriff and me. We have to clear the unit before five. Then the locks change. You can retrieve what's stored if you pay the back rent and the storage fee."

Behind him, one of the Rhino guys backed out of her doorway, her small dining table balanced on his shoulder. Another had her chair up-side down, hand wrapped around one of the legs Mara had tightened herself last winter when the screw stripped. The chair bumped the frame, and a chip of wood fell to the floor.

"Can I get my stuff?" Mara asked. Her voice sounded thin, like it belonged to someone standing farther down the stairs.

The manager sighed through his nose. "If you have a bag, you can take what you can carry. Everything else goes to storage or the landfill."

Storage or the landfill. The two options sat side by side in her mind, equal.

He stepped aside. She moved past him and into what used to be hers.

The first thing she noticed was the sound. The apartment had always been quiet: low buzz of the fridge, tick of the radiator. Now it was full of heavy breathing and tape tearing, the dull bump of wood against wall. Every noise was too loud for the small rooms.

Her end table was on its back, two legs already gone. The lamp that had sat on it lay sideways in a crate, shade bent, cord hanging over the edge. Kitchen cabinet doors gaped open. A man in work gloves scooped her plates and bowls by the armful into a black bin. One bowl slipped, hit the floor, and broke cleanly in two. He didn't look down.

In the bedroom, another man was taking her life in handfuls. He grabbed clothes from the dresser and closet without looking, T-shirts and socks, and the one decent dress, all mixed together, and shoved them into a trash bag. The bag bowed with each push, plastic whitening where it stretched.

Mara stood in the doorway and tried to make her mouth work. "Can I keep some of that?" she asked. "Please?"

The man didn't answer. He glanced at the hall, at the manager, then went back to the pile in front of him.

Mara stepped to the closet. Her winter boots were in the corner, still damp from the other day. She crouched, fingers clumsy on the laces, and dropped them into the canvas tote she used for groceries. The tote sagged under the weight. She then moved to the bookshelf.

Half the books were already gone, the bottom rows naked and dusty. A paperback lay on the floor, its spine cracked, pages fanned. She picked up three without looking at the titles, her hand shaking too much to choose. The tote pulled harder at her shoulder.

On the desk, her old phone charger lay coiled like something someone had meant to throw away. Next to it was the envelope with her birth certificate, corner bent. She grabbed both. For a second, she thought she saw one of the red rent envelopes under a stack of junk mail in a crate, but a gloved hand dropped a blender on top of it, and the white disappeared.

"Is that it?" the man in the bedroom asked. Without expression. Just needing to know if she was done being in his way.

"In a minute," she said, but her voice barely carried over the sound of tape ripping from a roll.

In the bathroom, the mirror was smeared with someone else's hands. Her toothbrush lay on the edge of the sink, wet from where it had been knocked over. She took it, and the nearly empty toothpaste, and the hairbrush missing half its bristles. There was nothing else that was hers.

Or there was, but she didn't have hands for it.

She went back to the living room. Two more men were there now, lifting the TV, her cheap one, the cord dangling. One paused when he saw her, eyes flicking to the tote, then to her face. For a second, he looked like he might say something. Then the other man said, "Lift," and he turned away.

Mara opened her mouth. She wanted to apologize for the mess. She wanted to tell them which drawers stuck, which shelves would come loose if they pulled too hard. She wanted to ask them to be careful with the things that weren't worth anything to anyone else.

Nothing came out.

"Time is up," the manager said behind her. His voice was softer now, but the words weren't. "We have to finish."

Mara nodded because there was nothing else to do. The tote strap cut into her shoulder. Her fingers had gone numb around it.

In the hall, she heard the clatter of her dishes as someone emptied a cabinet straight into a plastic bin. A fork hit the tile and skittered. One of the men made a joke about how light the place was, how she "traveled easy." The punchline got lost under the thump of a drawer being dumped, but the laughter didn't.

She went down the stairs. At 2A, the door was open a few inches. A woman in sweatpants stood inside with a beer in one hand and a cigarette in the other, watching. When their eyes met, the woman flinched and shut the door most of the way, leaving only a thin strip of light.

At the ground floor, Mara stepped outside into the raw air. The cold hit the damp at the corners of her eyes and made them sting. She leaned against the wall. The tote dragged her sideways.

Through the open window above, she could still hear them at it. A crash, then the sound of something metal rolling. Tape ripping. Someone saying, "Leave it. It's broken anyway." Each noise lined up in her chest and waited, like they were taking numbers.

After a while, the noises thinned out. The Rhino crew came out carrying her mattress. One of the men noticed her and looked for a second too long. Then he looked away and helped guide the mattress into the truck.

The property manager followed, collar turned up, clipboard hugged to his chest. He didn't look at Mara at all, but he knew she was there.

The truck door slid down with a final echoing slam. The sound shook dust from the bricks. Then it was just a building again, blank-faced to the street.

Mara stood on the sidewalk, the tote a dead weight against her side. Her keys were still in her pocket, hot from her hand. She closed her fingers around them until the edges bit into her palm, then let them go.

She turned away and walked. Her body moved first, then her mind, pulled along after it.

She didn't look back.

She walked until her legs hurt. The city was changing shift, daytime replaced by a different breed of movement: students with headphones, warehouse guys on smoke break, the first thin thread of evening commuters. Mara kept going, head down, the tote bag thumping against her ribs.

There was a shelter three blocks south, behind a church and beside a pay-to-park lot. Mara had seen it before, never needed it. She turned in and stepped through the glass door. The lobby was small and bright. The man at the desk looked up from his phone.

"Intake's at four," he said. "You're late."

Mara nodded, not trusting her voice.

He reached for a clipboard anyway. "You been here before?"

She shook her head.

He scanned the sheet. "We're full tonight. You can try the day center on Eighth; they don't do beds, just coffee and showers. If you come back early tomorrow, you might get a spot. That's the best I can do."

"Okay," Mara said.

The man offered a brief, tired smile. "You need a bus pass?"

"No. Thank you."

She left.

The cold was deeper now, sinking under her skin. She checked the time: 6:27 p.m. She wondered if Marcy had made it to the arcade after work, her favorite hangout.

Mara walked to the park at the end of the street, a patch of frozen grass and cold iron benches. She sat with her knees pulled up, hands deep in the pockets of her thin jacket. The tote was heavier with every passing minute.

She watched the city lights flicker on, one window at a time. She saw the street cleaners, the runners in neon vests, the slow float of the #12 bus down the avenue. She counted cars, not for any reason except to prove she could.

At some point, a young homeless man with a grocery cart passed by, then doubled back. He eyed her bag, then her face, and seemed to weigh the risk. Mara looked back at him, blank. He nodded once and pushed his cart away, metal wheels screeching on the pavement.

Mara sat until her legs lost feeling. The bench was cold and sharp against her back. She thought about standing, but the thought was too much.

She stared at the Tower in the distance, its windows bright even after hours. She counted floors by rows of light, fifty. She wondered if anyone in the building knew she was out here.

***

Sometime after midnight, the wind picked up with light rain. Mara dug deeper into her old, worn-out jacket. She tried to sleep, but her body resisted.

She let her mind drift. She imagined walking back to the café, letting herself in through the service door. She pictured herself behind the counter, making coffee, her hands steady again. She imagined the air inside: warm, dry, familiar.

The next morning, she would go back. Maybe Marcy would laugh and ask about her day. Maybe no one would say a word. Maybe no one would notice her wet, wrinkly uniform.

For now, she watched the Tower, its windows steady and indifferent against the night.

She held on to the image until the sky began to pale, and the world gave her another day.

Then Mara stood.

She shifted the tote strap higher on her shoulder, turned her body toward the Tower, and started walking before she could talk herself out of it.

CHAPTER FOUR

THE ACCESS BADGE

That morning, Mara slipped into the Tower by the service entrance, same as always. Her access badge caught the reader on the second try; the light blinked green, and the lock let go with a tired click. Her polo was wrinkled from the night on the park bench, the fabric creased at the shoulders and damp at the collar. She was early, though not by much. She steadied herself against the glass wall, smoothed the front of her shirt with the heel of her hand, then moved on.

The staff corridor was empty. Fluorescent strips flickered on, one by one. She moved on instinct, eyes down. The skin beneath her clothes was clammy, the fabric stiff where last night's rain hadn't dried. The only clean thing on her was the coffee-scented breath she'd stolen by huddling next to a bakery vent on the walk over.

In the staff bathroom, Mara splashed water on her face, pinched her cheeks, and scrubbed at the sleep lines in the corners of her mouth. The fluorescent mirror didn't flatter. She found a hair tie in her pocket and pulled her hair into a knot so tight it tugged at the corners of her scalp. She checked her uniform: shirt okay, pants okay, the lanyard still white and temporary. She leaned over the sink and watched the water run until her fingertips tingled.

She kept her head down as she keyed into the café. It was dim, peaceful, untouched except for the overnight chill. The espresso machine exhaled into the silence. Mara turned it on and listened for the rhythm of its heart: boiler, click, pause, repeat. She loaded pastries into the bins, checked milk levels, and rearranged cups so that the ones with the least visible stains went up front.

Marcy arrived at 5:56 a.m., hair still damp, the usual war paint swapped out for under-eye concealer applied with reckless energy. She blew in on the wind, a scrap of gossip about someone from compliance, her voice so loud it broke the silence.

"Morning, Flores. You look." Marcy paused, did a blink-scan, then skipped the comment. "You want to open, or should I?"

"I'll do it," Mara said.

The regulars filed in at 6:01 a.m., a cluster of men in navy suits and the maintenance guy with his orange travel mug. Mara took the orders and let her body remember how to move fast without thinking. The crowd was heavier than usual, or maybe it was just that she was so light: the calories of yesterday gone, and the ones from today not yet earned.

Marcy ran the bar, humming along to a playlist no one else could hear. She tamped espresso so hard the portafilter screamed, then pulled the shot in a single, unbroken stream. "You want to split the muffins now or wait until the nine o'clock crowd eats us alive?"

"Now's fine," Mara said.

Marcy leaned in, not quite whispering. "You sleep okay?"

"Fine."

"You sure?"

"Yeah." Mara's voice came out softer than she meant.

Marcy shrugged and started slicing banana bread with a plastic knife, her whole upper body involved in the motion.

The line snaked through the lobby. Mara kept her eyes on the register, the tap of the keys, the slow advance of the line. She could feel every irregularity in the floor tile through the thin soles of her shoes. There was a cut on her heel, raw and unhealed from walking all night, but she ignored it.

A man in a black turtleneck ordered three Americanos and one double cortado, then leaned over the bar to ask Marcy for "whatever's still warm." He glanced at Mara, not quite meeting her eyes, and handed over his loyalty card. His nails were bitten to the skin.

"Long night?" Marcy asked him.

He made a noise somewhere between a laugh and a cough. "Twelve hours on site. I'd kill to sleep in my own bed."

"Yeah," Mara said, too loudly.

He looked up, surprised by the sound, but then accepted his drinks and hurried off.

Marcy caught Mara's eye. "You're on edge today," she said.

Mara didn't answer. She could feel her hands shaking as she reached for the next cup.

By 7:00 a.m., the line thinned out. The sky outside was the color of over-brewed tea. Mara rang up a few more orders, restocked the milk, and wiped down the counter until it was so clean her reflection blurred into the surface. She found herself staring at the rippling version of her own face, then snapped out of it when Marcy elbowed her for a spoon.

The ache in her body was new. Not hunger exactly, more like an emptiness that radiated from her core to the tips of her fingers. Every part of her was cold, except where she touched the espresso machine or the steam wand; those spots burned.

Marcy started a conversation with a woman in a gray sweater about an office fantasy league. Mara only heard pieces.

"...so if you pick the wrong candidate, you have to bring donuts for the whole team. Like, your actual money on the line. Corporate hazing, but with more carbs."

The woman in the sweater laughed. "I'm just in it for the coffee. If I had to go without, I'd die."

Marcy leaned closer. "You'd be surprised what you can survive."

Mara drifted to the end of the counter and started stacking sleeves, each one rotated so the logo faced the counter. She let her mind blank out, focusing only on the texture of cardboard and the sound of the lobby's recycled air.

By 8:05 a.m., the rush was over. Marcy grabbed a scone and leaned against the bar, chewing with the contentment of someone who'd never skipped a meal in her life. Mara reset the pastry case and filled the sugar dispensers, wiping up every stray crystal.

"You want a break?" Marcy asked.

"I'm good."

Marcy squinted. "You look like you could use some sun."

Mara forced a smile. "I'll get some on my walk home."

Marcy shrugged, unconvinced, and popped the last of the scone into her mouth.

Mara made it through the next hour by holding to the ritual: check the time, refill the syrups, count the lids. There was comfort in knowing exactly what was next, in the predictability of the machine. She watched the minutes pass on the wall clock, wishing herself forward.

At 9:21 a.m., Mara finally slipped away, telling Marcy she had to use the bathroom. She walked past the staff lounge, empty, lights off, and out into the corridor that led to the indoor garden.

It wasn't a real garden, just a sunken patch of earth ringed with potted ferns and a few anemic shrubs. The benches were plastic, made to look like wood, the kind with slats wide enough to leave red stripes on your legs. The light was artificial too, meant to mimic the sun. It buzzed at a frequency just outside hearing range, but Mara could feel it behind her eyes.

She sat on the low stone wall and let her head drop back.

The warmth on her face felt like permission. She closed her eyes and counted to one hundred, letting the heat soak in. For a few seconds, she could imagine staying right here forever, curled behind plastic leaves, hidden in the one place inside the Tower that pretended it wasn't watching.

A cleaner in a blue polo swept the brick path, ignoring her with professional courtesy. Mara kept her head low anyway. She hadn't come here for air. She'd come here to avoid the staff room, where she might have cried.

Her brain played the eviction scene on loop: orange vests, gloved hands, the way her entire life had been reduced to a tote bag and three books.

She opened her eyes and stared at the mulch.

Along the edge, it had been combed into straight lines. Near the base of one shrub, a section looked disturbed, brown pushed slightly out of pattern. Something dull and metallic sat there, mostly buried, catching the light in a way the plastic leaves didn't.

Mara leaned forward and brushed the mulch aside with her fingers.

A corner of plastic. Grimy. Worn.

She worked it free and wiped it on her pant leg.

It was an access badge, the kind everyone in the building wore. The plastic was scuffed, the name half-faded by months of abrasion. She squinted at the photo. The woman's face was young, dark hair pulled back, eyes set with a tension Mara recognized. The resemblance was enough that, on a passing glance, you might swap one for the other.

A. Morales.

Underneath, simply read "Special Projects."

Mara looked up. The cleaner had moved to the far end of the garden, sweeping in slow, determined strokes. No one else was in sight. Mara turned the badge over. Old adhesive clung to the back where a lanyard had once been, tacky and unpleasant.

She stared at it longer than she meant to, then stood and walked toward the maintenance door. A metal access panel sat beside it, scratched and dull from years of use. She felt stupid, but she swiped the badge anyway.

The light flashed green.

A small rush of air hissed behind the door, and for a moment Mara stood motionless, heart thudding. She pulled the badge back and looked at the photo again, like the face might have changed.

The cleaner's broom scraped closer. Mara slid the access badge into her apron pocket, the edge biting into her thigh, and turned away before she could talk herself into doing something polite.

She walked the perimeter of the garden once, then twice, keeping her hands in her pockets so she wouldn't reach for it again. Her own access badge was white with no real access. She could barely open the café's supply closet without being buzzed in by a supervisor.

This card, though.

Special Projects.

Power, or the illusion of it. She tried to imagine a situation where she'd need it and came up blank. Still, she kept her hand over her apron pocket like it might run off without her.

Return it to Security, a thought offered.

Then it left.

She headed back toward the café, the access badge a secret weight against her skin. As she walked, she traced the letters with her thumb, memorizing the shape of the name.

A. Morales.

She didn't know what she was going to do. But the idea of having a key to somewhere, anywhere, felt less like hope than it should have.

She clocked back in, washed her hands for a full thirty seconds, and got back to work. The line was already forming again. Marcy waved her over.

"You all right?" Marcy asked, low.

"Yeah," Mara said, and it was almost true.

She kept her hand in her apron pocket, the access badge pressing hard against her skin.

***

She worked the rest of the day on habit alone, the access badge a constant reminder against her skin. By the time she clocked out, it felt less like something she'd found than something that expected her to come back.

She left through the staff corridor and walked until the Tower's glass was behind her. The streets were busy in the way they always were at the end of her shift, but it all sounded muffled, like someone had turned the city down.

She walked back to the small park with benches bolted to the concrete. The first one she tried was wet, and the second was colder. She sat anyway. Her thin jacket clung to her shoulders. Water crept down the back of her collar and pooled at her waistband. Time passed in small, stupid measurements: headlights, footsteps, the hiss of a bus kneeling at the curb. She thought about calling her brother, two time zones away, thumb hovering over his name, then put the phone back in her pocket. He's probably busy anyway.

She kept the Morales access badge in her fist, thumb rubbing the raised letters until they felt familiar. She tried to picture a safe place to spend the night and came up with nothing that didn't end with her waking up to someone's boot near her bag. The bench pulled heat out of her in slow, steady draws, and she caught herself nodding once, twice. If she fell asleep like this, cold and wet, she might not wake up. She leaned forward, elbows on her knees, and watched her breath bloom and vanish. Her body had started to do that quiet shiver that wasn't exactly cold anymore, just her system running out of options. She stayed awake anyway, blinking hard, letting the minutes drag past. The park lights buzzed overhead. A bus hissed at the curb and pulled away. People passed without looking at her face.

***

By the time full dark settled, Mara had drifted back toward the Tower without quite deciding to. The city was louder than it had been in the morning, but the noise felt far away, like it belonged to someone else.

The Tower felt different when it thought no one was watching. The lobby lights were down to half, enough to keep the marble from vanishing, not enough to flatter anyone. The revolving doors sat still. Exit signs glowed in narrow red strips, the only color in a room that had forgotten the day.

Mara stood across the street with her hands jammed in her pockets and the Morales access badge pressed against her palm. Rain found the back of her neck where her collar never quite closed. Her socks were still damp. The cold had leeched into her bones in a way the first night outside hadn't.

She closed her eyes and ran the math she kept pretending she was done with. Rent gone. Pills that cost more than food. One part-time job that barely covered anything when she had a door to lock behind her. Lose the job, and the numbers didn't go bad. They disappeared.

Outside was more of last night. Bus benches if she was early, nothing if she was late. Shelter waitlists. Cops who didn't like loitering. Her body failing slowly, then quickly.

Inside was heat. Dry clothes. A place to lie down that wasn't wet.

Also trespass. Termination. Security calling the cops. Her name on a report she'd never see: UNAUTHORIZED ACCESS. STAFF MIS-CONDUCT.

Her fingers tightened around the access badge until the cracked corner bit into her skin.

Her mother's voice arrived the way it always did when Mara was about to do something bad: *We don't take what isn't ours. We don't give them a reason. Don't steal. Don't lie. Don't make noise.*

Her father, folding a bus map with thick fingers, said: *Be inside, not out.*

Inside meant a desk back then. A chair. An access badge with her own face.

The access badge in her palm was both things at once: theft and invitation. It belonged to someone else. It belonged to the building. It didn't belong to the woman standing in the rain trying to decide which rule mattered more.

She opened her eyes. She could barely see her old apartment building in the distance. No light in her window. No furniture left to imagine.

The truck had taken the last of that away. There was nothing to go back to that wasn't a blank wall.

The Tower, by comparison, looked awake even on half power. Vents breathed. Somewhere, an elevator shifted in its shaft. The building didn't know she was outside. It didn't know she wasn't supposed to be inside.

She pictured the morning. Walking into work half-frozen, hands shaking so badly she'd drop cups, burn herself, get sent home early, lose shifts, lose the only paycheck that still had her name on it. The Tower would keep breathing. It wouldn't notice the difference between a tired barista and no barista at all.

She pictured Security catching her instead. A hand on her arm. A printout on a desk. Rick from the GSOC replaying footage she couldn't argue with. The door behind her closing harder than the one in her apartment ever had.

Two futures. Both bad.

She could almost hear her mother again: *We came to America so you wouldn't have to hide.* And Mara knew what she meant. *Step through the door. Don't stand there.*

This is only temporary, Mara said under her breath. Temporary homeless. Temporary access badge thief. Temporary everything. She didn't believe it, but she needed something to call this version of herself.

She breathed once, then again, steadying it the way she did before carrying a full tray across the lobby. The street between her and the Tower was only a few painted lines and thirty feet of wet asphalt, but it felt like the space between two lives.

She crossed.

The plaza tiles were colder than the sidewalk. The glass doors loomed taller from this side. Her own access badge would have been dead by now. This one was a stranger's, found in garden dirt like trash.

She lifted it to the reader.

For a heartbeat, nothing happened.

Then the light turned green, calm as it did at five in the morning, as if the Tower couldn't tell the difference between a shift and a trespass. The lock clicked open with the same precise sound.

"Please step into the door," the automated voice said.

Inside, the lobby was all shadow and shine. The marble floor reflected strips of emergency light and the red glow from exit signs. The revolving doors sat still. The reception desk was empty, just two monitors glowing in sleep mode. The air smelled of wet stone and faint chemical lemon.

Her footsteps echoed too loudly. She slowed them.

Habit pulled her to the café gate first. The gate was down and locked, silver teeth interlaced. Her own access badge wouldn't help. She lifted the Special Projects access badge instead and touched it to the reader.

Green.

The gate unlatched with a single, precise click. For a second, she waited, expecting an alarm or a voice. Nothing. Just the low buzz of compressors and the soft tick of cooling metal.

She ducked under, lowered the gate behind her until it sat just above her shoulder, the way they left it when moving heavy boxes. From the lobby, the café would look closed. From inside, the machines gleamed faintly under the red exit light. The espresso machine was a dark bulk, warm even in sleep. The smell of burnt sugar still clung to the air.

"This is temporary," she told the machines, because someone should hear it.

She didn't try to sleep here. Too exposed. Too easy to find. The Tower was full of places nobody bothered to look at.

The service corridor beyond the café was colder. Fluorescent strips buzzed and flattened everything to a tired white. The freight elevator call button glowed a faint yellow. When she pressed it, she felt the vibration deep below, the slow movement of weight and cable.

The doors parted without a sound.

Inside, the air smelled of oil and metal polish. She stepped in, thumb grazing the edge of the access badge through her pocket. The panel ran from B1 to 15, each button a promise or a warning.

She randomly chose seven.

The elevator climbed with a steady pull. Floor numbers blinked in sequence: two, three, four, five... Her reflection swam in the brushed steel, stretched and blurred. She didn't look directly at it. At seven, the elevator sighed to a stop.

The doors opened on an unfinished floor.

Plastic sheeting hung from the ceiling in strips. Stacks of drywall leaned against the walls, their ends wrapped in cloudy plastic. Paint cans sat in a line, lids crusted with dried color. The air smelled of dust and cold plaster. Somewhere, a drip echoed, amplified by emptiness.

She stepped out and listened.

No voices. No vents pushing cafeteria smells. No printer whine, no elevator chime. Just the building's skeleton: an occasional creak, a faint hiss in the pipes, a distant mechanical breath.

A work lamp glowed near the windows, clamped to a metal stand. Its cord snaked across the floor to an outlet that didn't look trustworthy. The light cast a soft circle of gold on concrete and dust.

She walked to the massive glass windows.

The city below was spread out like circuitry, streets thin and glowing, the river a dark line cutting through. The Tower's reflection hung faintly over it all, a ghost of the building drawn over the real one.

She pressed her palm against the glass. It was cold enough to make her bones ache. When she lifted her hand, the print faded almost immediately.

In the far corner, a roll of old wallpaper lay half-unfurled, edges curled, with a fallen sheet of plastic draped over it beside a stack of drywall. She dragged them closer to the wall, into a gap behind the drywall where the light from the hall couldn't quite reach. She spread the wallpaper flat as a makeshift mat and eased herself down onto it. The paper crackled under her weight. It smelled like glue and mildew, sharp in the cold air.

The chill came up through the concrete in a slow, heavy climb. She curled on her side and pulled the plastic over her legs. It tore at the edge but held enough to take the sting off the air. The word temporary bit the inside of her mouth.

She whispered it anyway. "Temporary."

Above her, the unfinished ceiling showed beams and pipes in exposed lines. Light from the work lamp caught small bits of metal, made them wink, and then disappear. Somewhere far below, a door closed with a muffled thud. Vibration traveled up the frame and into her shoulders.

Tears came without drama, without noise. They slid sideways into her hair, where the dust caught them. She wiped her face with the heel of her hand, annoyed at herself. This wasn't what she'd planned. There was no plan now.

Her parents would have had something to say about all of this. Mara kept running that line in her head, as if it might change.

She lay there, eyes open, until the night started to thin at the edges. The lamp clicked once and burned a little warmer, reacting to some timed command. The cold never really left. Her body just got used to it.

   She didn't sleep, not much anyway.

CHAPTER FIVE

MAPPING THE MACHINE

When Mara finally drifted off, her alarm snapped her awake. She woke in her corner on the seventh floor, wrapped in plastic sheeting and fiberglass dust. She'd burrowed deep into the space behind a stack of drywall, shoving her bag and shoes against the wall so the light couldn't catch them from the construction hall. She was shivering, but only noticed it when her jaw started to click.

Her phone, set face down on the unfinished floor, vibrated with the alarm. She silenced it after half a second, then sat up, rubbing the pins and needles from her calves. The only sound was the buzz of the HVAC and, somewhere distant, the rhythmic slap of a cleaning crew mopping tile. She checked the time: 4:21 a.m.

The first rule was never to be caught out of place. Mara rolled up her makeshift blanket, shook drywall dust out of her hair, and checked the gap between the drywall stack and the column. Nothing had shifted overnight. No footprints, no wrappers, no sign anyone else had come this way. She pulled her jacket tight, wiped her face with the hem of her sleeve, and let her pulse settle.

The restroom on this floor was off-limits now; she'd seen the electricians entering the seventh floor a few days ago when she was delivering coffee and pastries on the eighth floor. She would need to make it down to the staff restrooms on the third floor without being seen, or at least without being remembered. There was an art to moving through the Tower before it woke, timing the motion sensors, using the service stairwells that the overnight crews ignored, pausing at each landing to check for voices or light.

Her shoes made no noise on the raw concrete. She crept to the exit and pressed her ear to the door. The corridor outside was silent. She slid the door open just enough to slip through, then walked flat-footed down the hall, head down. The elevator wasn't an option; the elevator logged every floor, and the cameras would catch her face. Stairs only. She took them two at a time, knees aching, until she reached the third floor.

On the landing, she waited. The only motion was a faint ripple of light under the door, from an early cleaner, maybe, or security doing a sweep. Mara braced herself, counted to ten, and opened the door.

The staff hallway was empty except for the faint blue of the vending machine, a large printer blinking red, and the half-lit exit sign at the far end. As she walked past the printer, Mara gave the side of the casing a sharp slap without breaking stride. The red blink stuttered, flipped to green, and the machine shuddered awake, spitting out a backlog of pages. Once at the restroom, she nudged the door open with her shoulder and slid inside.

The mirror was unforgiving. She looked sallow, jaw set, hair standing out in every direction. She splashed water on her face, scrubbed it dry with a brown paper towel, then set to work fixing her hair. She didn't have a brush, so she combed it with her fingers, pulling it back into a bun as tight as her skin would bear. She patted her cheeks, pinched color into them, and checked her teeth. The line of her jaw trembled, just a little, but she ignored it.

She tried to smooth out the wrinkles in her shirt, but most remained. She rolled her sleeves. She checked herself in the mirror. It would have to do.

A woman in a blue cleaning smock entered, pushing a cart loaded with bleach and rags. Mara nodded, gave a practiced half-smile, then stepped aside. The woman didn't look at her face; her gaze hovered just over Mara's shoulder, as if seeing her in the reflection and nowhere else. Mara dried her hands, wiped down the edge of the sink, and slipped out, leaving no trace.

She took the back hall to the lobby, keeping close to the wall where the security cameras would catch only the top of her head. She passed a security guard at the end of the corridor, tall, with a nervous tap of his right foot, badge half-visible in the dim light. He didn't stop her, just nodded, eyes glazed with lack of sleep. She was just another worker on her way to open.

The lobby lights were coming up in slow increments, the main floor still shadowed, but the café already buzzing with the pretense of energy. She slipped behind the counter and started the espresso machine. The sound was a comfort; it was something she could control.

She checked the pastries, restocked the milk, and lined up the coffee cups so the logo faced out. The movements were automatic, but this morning she caught herself watching her hands, making sure they didn't shake.

At 6:01 a.m., the first regular wandered up to the entrance, peering inside as if expecting her. Mara flipped the gate up and gave him a nod. He ordered the usual, drip, black, two sugars, no sleeve, and paid in cash.

"Early today," he said.

"Had to get a head start," Mara replied, voice steady.

He smiled, took his cup, and walked to his spot by the window.

Marcy arrived ten minutes later, hair damp, sleeves rolled, a scuff of mascara on her cheek. "Sorry, I'm late. An hour late. I'll make it up." In an attempt to change the subject, Marcy asked, "You okay?"

"Couldn't sleep," Mara said.

"Welcome to the club." Marcy tied on her apron, already gossiping about people at the arcade.

Mara poured herself a shot, drank it standing, and wiped down the bar until it shone. She checked her phone. Nothing new. She deleted three notifications without reading them, then tucked the phone deep in her pocket.

The lobby brightened. People trickled in, some in clusters, some alone. Mara greeted each one the same way, keeping her voice calm, her expression unreadable. By 6:30 a.m., the rush began. She moved through it with the same precision as always, but today there was a fraction less effort, a fraction less pretense.

She was still here. That was enough.

By the time the sun rose, Mara had found her rhythm. She smiled at the regulars, ignored the ones who tried to make small talk, and kept the line moving. She was a fixture, invisible as always. Just another worker, in the heart of the Tower.

Nobody asked where she'd come from, or where she'd go when the shift ended.

Behind the counter, uniform now perfect, hair pinned tight, Mara blended into the machinery of the building, and nobody saw the difference.

***

The lobby café existed on two separate clocks. The customer clock arrived in half-hour surges, each wave hungry and impatient. The building's clock ran deeper, visible only if you watched for it. Mara watched for it now, because she had to.

By 7:05 a.m., the line was six deep. Marcy was in rare form, pulling shots with both hands, her chatter two octaves above normal.

"Next," Mara called, setting the tempo.

A woman with a rigid bun and a glossy phone case ordered a latte without looking up. Mara logged the time anyway. 7:06 a.m., which meant Legal.

In the breaks between orders, Mara tracked movement instead of faces. Security drifted in loops. Cleaning crews moved in waves. Mail runners cut through at consistent minutes. The main lobby doors always stuck for a second at 8:13 a.m., long enough to create a pause people mistook for their own hesitation.

The tells were in the hands. A nail chewed raw. A knuckle popped before swiping a card. A thumb hovering near an access badge like it could be used as a shield. Mara took it in without staring.

At 7:18 a.m., Sammy appeared in his blue coveralls, thermos dangling from two fingers. He bypassed the line, gave Marcy a two-finger salute, and caught Mara's eye with a tilt of his head.

"Morning," she said.

He nodded. "How's the machinery?"

"Running hot, but not boiling over yet."

Sammy leaned in. "If the hopper starts clumping, back off by a quarter turn. New batch. It tastes different."

"Figures," Mara said. She watched his eyes for a flicker of recognition, any sign he knew more than he was saying, but he just sipped from his thermos and turned toward the freight elevator.

At 7:23 a.m., the first delivery arrived. Mara met the guy at the side door, signed the slip with her left hand, and counted cartons as he unloaded. The door behind him didn't close all the way. A wedge of light cut across the pastry case glass at a clean angle. For a second, Mara could see the reflection of the service corridor and the security guard posted there.

A blind spot in how the building assumed people stood.

Mara reset the counter, topped off syrups, and watched the guard's sweep without looking like she was watching. Every six minutes, the same loop. East entrance, staff corridor, main desk. He never lifted his head unless a voice rose above the background.

When her break came, Mara slipped out and walked a slow loop of the lobby, moving like someone killing time. Digital bulletin screens. A trash can. The ATM. Her reflection in the glass.

Security never glanced her way.

She filed three facts and held them close. Cameras overlapped but left thin gaps at corners. Cleaning started east and moved west like a tide. Stairwell doors required an access badge, but people held them without thinking when the person behind looked like they belonged.

That was the machine. Confident enough.

At 8:12 a.m., Janis appeared, mop bucket rolling, eyes already scanning for anything out of place. Mara admired the economy of Janis's movements, the way she avoided the main traffic until the lobby was clear, the way she stood for exactly twenty seconds after mopping to let the floor dry, never less, never more. Janis nodded at Mara as she passed, a flicker of recognition.

"Morning," Janis said, barely above a whisper.

"Morning," Mara replied, voice soft.

Janis stopped, glanced at the pastry case, then at Mara. "You ever notice how the bosses always order decaf, but none of them actually drink it?"

Mara smiled. "I pour half down the drain every day."

Janis grunted, then moved on. Mara watched her until she was out of sight, then returned to the counter.

***

The mid-morning lull was the best time for experiments. Mara set the auto-brewer to a two-minute delay, then slipped out the side entrance and up the service stairs. On three, she timed her walk past the security camera, four seconds from the door to the janitor's closet, just long enough to duck inside if anyone followed.

She listened for footsteps, heard none, then kept going. On five, she found the back hallway that ran parallel to the offices. The glass wall here was partially mirrored, but if you angled your body right, you could see into the HR bullpen without being seen yourself. She watched the HR staff move through their routines, the same three people walking out for their smoke break at exactly 10:04 a.m., every day.

On the way back, Mara tested a theory: if you pushed the fire door at the end of the hall, did the alarm trip? She pressed, just enough to make the latch click, then waited. Nothing. She let the door close, then took the stairs back to the lobby.

At her station, Marcy was finishing a phone call, eyebrows raised. "Hey, can you cover the bar for five? I gotta run to Security; they need me to sign for a package."

"Sure," Mara said, switching places.

Mara kept her eyes on the lobby. The security guard was at the far end now, flirting with a woman in a red blazer. Mara watched the way he tilted his head, the way his hand hovered near his badge. He was distracted. The line of sight from the café to the service corridor was clear, and the line for coffee was gone.

She decided to try again. Mara flipped the little sign to BACK IN 2 MINUTES, then ducked out the back and made a quick dash for the copy center.

Halfway there, a radio chirped from the corridor ahead. Mara froze behind a column, breath held, listening. Footsteps came closer, then slowed. A security guard paused at the corner and looked down the hall like he had forgotten why he'd turned.

Mara kept her face turned toward the wall, a person studying a bulletin she couldn't see.

The guard's hand hovered near his badge, then dropped. He walked on.

When the footsteps faded, Mara moved again, faster now, because the two minutes weren't a promise. They were a risk.

She stood by the supply closet, counted to ten, then slipped back to the café and turned the sign around again.

The rest of the shift passed in the same way, routine interrupted by small, controlled risks. Mara moved objects on the counter, just to see if anyone noticed. She let a napkin drift to the floor near the guard's post and watched as it sat for fifteen minutes before anyone picked it up, proof that the cameras weren't watching what they claimed to watch.

At 1:17 p.m., Sammy returned, toolbox in hand. He gave Mara a look, then set the box on the counter.

"Machine giving you trouble?"

"No, but the grinder's off by half a turn," she said.

He smiled, pleased. "You're good at this," he said, and she caught the double meaning.

She nodded. "It's all about observation."

He gave her a slow, assessing look. "You ever think about working upstairs?"

She shrugged, unsure if it was a joke.

"You'd get bored," Sammy said, "but you'd see everything."

***

At closing, she wiped down the bar, restocked the lids, and checked the pastry case one last time. She glanced at the security desk, saw the guard watching the doors, and noted the exact second he looked away.

She made a new list in her head, assembling the day's data points: the mailroom corridor was invisible from both cameras if you took the inner path by the copy center; the service stairs on two lagged by three seconds after badging in, enough to slip through with the right timing; Janis parked her cart outside the break room at 12:40 p.m., which meant the hallway was clear for at least five minutes.

She was building a map of the Tower's soft spots. Its indifferences, its glitches. It was a habit of ignoring anything that didn't match the pattern.

Tomorrow she'd test something bigger.

For now, she stayed where she belonged. She reset the counter, topped off the sleeves, and lined the cups so the logo faced out. In the glass of the pastry case, she caught her own reflection: calm, composed, a perfect copy of every other worker in the building. But inside, she was already planning the next move.

***

By closing, the lobby had thinned to echoes and meetings. Closing shift felt like theater. The script never changed. Marcy counted out the register, cracked a joke about "creative accounting," and scribbled her initials in the closing log. Mara wiped down the counter, stacked the chairs, and pretended not to watch the clock.

"Big plans tonight?" Marcy asked, pulling on her parka.

"Sleep," Mara said. "You?"

"Arcade. I'm gonna break my own record, or die trying." Marcy grinned, gave a two-finger salute, and bounced out through the staff exit.

Mara waited until she heard the outer door bang shut. Then she straightened her sleeves, checked her pockets, and slipped the A. Morales access badge from the front pocket of her pants, hidden under her apron.

She walked out of the café with a purpose, head up, stride confident. The cameras would catch her, but only as another worker heading home for the day. She made it to the far end of the lobby, ducked into the hallway, and instead of turning for the staff exit, veered toward the east stairwell.

The trick was to never look lost.

She took the stairs to two, pausing on the landing to listen. The floors above buzzed with work: contractors finishing a buildout, someone in Facilities banging on ductwork. On two, the hallway was bright, but the green light on the access badge reader pulsed every few seconds, like a distant heartbeat.

She swiped the Morales access badge. The reader beeped; the door unlocked.

Inside was the low buzz of machinery, the faint scent of ozone and lubricant. The walls were lined with pipes, electrical conduit, the kind of exposed utility guts no one ever cleaned. Mara walked the length of the hall, counting her steps, noting every junction and branching corridor.

The service doors here were a mixed bag. Some unlocked with the access badge, others resisted, maybe because they were tied to a different access level, or maybe just jammed by years of neglect. Mara tried them all, never staying long enough to draw attention.

At the midpoint of the hall, she reached a junction: left to the elevator equipment room, right to the riser closet, straight ahead to an unlabeled steel door. She listened at each, then pushed forward.

The access badge worked on the steel door. It opened onto a landing with two more doors and a grated window looking out over the building's inner shaft. She stepped through, careful to avoid the motion sensor above the frame. The floor here vibrated, not quite in rhythm with her heart but close enough to make her anxious.

She walked the perimeter, mapping the turns, checking the corners for cameras. She found a dead zone: a strip of wall just inside the riser closet, invisible from any lens she could spot.

She made a mental note, then left the way she'd come, closing the door gently.

On her way back, she almost ran into Janis.

The janitor was coming up the other direction, mop cart rolling slowly, eyes focused on the scuffed floor in front of her. For a split second, Mara froze, caught mid-step, but Janis didn't break stride.

Janis looked up, met Mara's gaze, then kept moving. At the last second, she angled her cart to block the line of sight from the corner camera, giving Mara a five-second window to pass behind her.

Mara did, shoulders tight, exhaling only when she was around the next bend.

She ducked into the stairwell, descended to the lower level, and found the building's main utility substation. The access badge worked here, too. Inside was a labyrinth of transformers, electrical panels, and storage shelves stacked with boxes no one had dusted since Y2K. Mara moved through it, breathing shallow, memorizing the rows and labels.

She left a test: moved a box from the bottom shelf to the top, rotated a clipboard so its logo faced away. A silent experiment. Would anyone notice?

On her way back, she checked the loading dock. The security guard was stationed at the end of the ramp, watching a tiny TV propped on a stack of pallets. Mara hugged the shadows, keeping to the wall where the light didn't reach. The guard never looked up.

By the time she returned to the stairwell, her pulse had leveled out. She ascended to five, found another service door, and tried the access badge. This one beeped yellow, denied. She held it a second longer. Nothing.

She heard voices behind her and ducked into the gap between the door and a row of stacked cardboard boxes. Two men in Facilities polos walked past, mid-argument about an HVAC ticket. Mara held her breath until their voices faded.

She tried the access badge on every door up to twelve. Some worked, some didn't. On eight, she found a narrow access hall lined with what looked like old IT hardware, most of it powered off. There was a utility sink, a folding chair, and a battered metal cabinet. Mara checked the cabinet: unlocked. Inside were cleaning supplies, a first aid kit, and a single high-visibility vest. She noted the contents and closed the cabinet.

She exited through the stairwell, skipping every other step, and looped back down to seven. She checked her hiding place behind the drywall. Everything was just as she'd left it.

She sat, heart still thudding, and took a moment to process.

Someone had seen her: Janis, but nothing had happened. No alarm, no pursuit. Instead, a gap was opened, a brief window of safety. A silent alliance.

Mara knew then that she wasn't the first to move unnoticed through these halls. The building was full of ghosts, each one watching out for the others, all of them invisible to the eyes that mattered.

She checked her phone. One text from Marcy: "I beat my high score!" Mara smiled.

She closed her eyes, replaying the path she'd taken, every twist and turn, every door that opened and every one that stayed shut.

She mapped the whole night in her mind.

When she finally drifted off, it was to the sound of the building's heartbeat, steady, unbroken, and just a little bit out of rhythm.

***

Mara didn't adapt the way people liked to imagine they would. Repetition did it. Same motions, day after day, until the strangeness wore off.

By the third night, she could sleep on concrete and wake without panic, jaw clenched against the cold, hands already moving. She kept her corner cleaner than the construction zone deserved. Cardboard flattened. Plastic folded. Shoes placed where they would not scrape. Nothing left behind that could become a question.

She stopped thinking of it as hiding and started thinking of it as procedure. If she followed procedure, she stayed employed. If she stayed employed, she stayed alive.

The hardest part was the hours. Midnight to four was an ocean of static and fluorescent buzz, the building's systems breathing around her. She filled the time the way she filled the café. Inventory. Timing. Routes.

What changed when the hallway was empty. What changed when it wasn't.

On her second Friday, she risked a shower in the gym locker room. She waited until the cleaning crew finished, then slipped in behind a group from Sales who stumbled through the door laughing too loudly and smelling like tequila. She scrubbed drywall dust from her skin, stole a squirt of someone's expensive body wash, and dried off with abrasive paper towels that felt like punishment.

When she came out, she almost ran into Janis again.

The janitor stood by the sinks, scrolling through a crossword app, mop cart parked as it belonged there. She looked up, registered Mara in a glance, then returned to the puzzle without changing her face.

Mara nodded once.

Janis nodded back.

Recognition.

Mara went back to seven with damp hair and a steadier pulse. She lay down behind the drywall stack and listened to the Tower settle. Somewhere far below, a door latched. Somewhere above, an elevator moved. The building kept working, and so did she.

CHAPTER SIX

THE TOWER'S VEINS

Mornings in the Tower ran on muscle memory. By 8:00 a.m., the line at the café was down to three, all of them regulars. Marcy handled the register, her voice rising above the drone of the espresso machine, pulling laughs from the office crowd. Mara kept to the bar, dosing shots, steaming milk, and keeping the counter so spotless it reflected her hands in double.

Sammy showed up at 8:12 a.m. He always looked as if he'd just finished a twelve-hour shift, coveralls half-zipped, T-shirt stained with oil in lines that traced out a day's movement. His thermos was tucked under one arm, battered enough to pass as an antique. He paused at the end of the counter, waiting for the line to collapse on itself.

When it did, he nodded at Mara. "Just coffee. No need to fix it."

"Rough night?" she said, voice quiet enough that only he would catch it.

Sammy snorted. "Is it ever not?"

She poured him a drip, black, and slid it across the bar. He stood off to the side, sipping while he watched the lobby cycle through its phases.

Analysts passed by, eyes fixed on their screens. The mail guy ran his cart over the same patch of tile four times before lifting it bodily over the seam. A suit from HR wiped donut glaze from her phone, glancing up just long enough to see Sammy and then look away.

Marcy called over, "Hey, you gonna fix the vending machine or what?"

Sammy grinned without turning. "You mean the coin-eating, button-sticking, corporate morale destroyer?"

"The one and only."

"Work order's been open since last year."

Marcy shook her head, rolling her eyes at Mara. "Can't get good help these days."

Sammy drifted closer to the bar, dropped his voice. "You wanna know the real problem? The only things that ever get fixed are the things that make money. Everything else is duct tape and a wish." He looked at Mara as if daring her to disagree.

She didn't. She pulled a rag from the sanitizing bucket and wiped down the steel edge of the bar. "So what's broken today?"

He counted off on his fingers. "Two freight elevators stuck in override. Dock doors cycling at random. Hot water loop on eleven is dead. Again. Security's got a camera out in the west stairwell, but they don't care because it's a blind spot no one ever checks."

Mara let the words settle. Failures. Gaps.

"You ever get sick of being the only person who knows how this place works?" she asked.

Sammy looked surprised, then laughed once, short and breathy. "I'm not the only one. You know more than you let on."

"I just watch," she said.

"Same skill set," he replied. "Same outcomes." He ran a hand through his hair. "You ever been inside a freight elevator when it stalls?"

"No."

"It's like being in a casket with fluorescent lights. You start hearing things. Pipes ticking. The building settling. Makes you realize how much of this place is held together by timing."

Marcy glided over, dropping a plastic-wrapped Danish on the bar. "This one's on the house. For emotional support."

Sammy pocketed it. "You want the secret to the whole building?"

"Tell me."

"It's the veins," he said, tapping the countertop. "Freight elevators. Loading docks. Service tunnels. Everything that matters moves through them. Shut those down, and the Tower's dead in a day."

Mara folded a towel under the bar. "Isn't that true anywhere?"

"Not like this." He leaned closer. "They built it so nobody ever has to see anyone else. Executives, staff, janitors, deliveries. Separate paths. Separate worlds. But the freight?" He nodded toward the back corridor. "That goes everywhere."

Marcy pretended to yawn. "You two are so intense. I'm getting existential just listening."

Sammy finished his coffee. "Dock supervisor gets antsy if I'm late." He gave a two-finger salute and disappeared down the service hall.

Marcy watched him go. "He always looks like he's halfway out of the building."

Mara rinsed a coffee pot. "Maybe he is."

Marcy grinned. "You ever think about running away? Just walking out and never coming back?"

"All the time," Mara said, and didn't smile.

They worked the next stretch in near silence. Mara found herself tracking the lobby again, picturing the veins Sammy had described. If the freight went everywhere, then so could she.

***

When the lull hit at 10:00 a.m., Marcy opened the fridge and swore. "We're almost out of oat milk."

Mara already knew. One carton and a half.

"I'll grab more," she said.

"Please," Marcy said. "We've got a meeting crowd coming in, and I'm not fighting about dairy."

Mara took the empty crate and the service key and headed out back.

The corridor marked SERVICE – NO PUBLIC ACCESS was bright and empty. She moved with purpose, crate balanced on her hip, stride even. Walk as you belong. Don't study. Don't hesitate.

The fire doors opened onto the loading dock, and the air hit her cold and metallic. Diesel rumble. Forklift shriek. The dull slam of pallets.

A man in a neon vest leaned against the wall scrolling his phone. He flicked his eyes up at Mara, registered the crate, and went back to the screen.

The freight elevator bay sat at the far end. Three wide doors. Cracked concrete. Peeling caution tape. No camera pointed directly at the elevator doors, only one angled toward the ramp.

The middle elevator dinged and opened for no one.

The lights inside flickered.

The elevator shuddered and stalled for a second too long.

Mara stopped walking.

Casket with fluorescent lights.

The elevator roared again, as if embarrassed, and continued its cycle. The doors stayed open. Nothing else happened.

She forced her breath steady and stepped closer, pretending to read the ELEVATOR RULES sign.

A radio crackled behind her.

"Dock spot check in progress. Access badge compliance. West corridor to freight."

Mara didn't turn.

This wasn't the moment to observe. This was the moment to commit.

She adjusted her grip on the crate, shifted her posture, and became exactly what she looked like: a worker on an errand. Not rushed. Not curious. Just passing through.

She walked past the elevator and into the cooler.

The door stuck. She yanked it open, grabbed two cartons of oat milk, and didn't linger. When she came back out, the radio was still muttering somewhere behind her. Footsteps echoed down the dock.

She crossed the bay at a steady pace, nodded once at the neon-vested man, and pushed through the fire doors without looking back.

Only in the corridor did her pulse catch up with her.

Back in the café, Marcy took the cartons with visible relief. "You're a hero."

Mara slid the crate under the prep table. "It's all there if you know where to look."

She meant more than oat milk.

The rest of the shift passed quietly. Mara worked the bar, but her attention kept drifting toward the loading dock. The sound of elevators. The idea that some paths weren't meant to be seen.

***

At closing, she wiped down the counter and waited until Marcy left.

Then she took the service stairs up to the seventh floor, moving only when the corridors went quiet.

CHAPTER SEVEN

RUMORS IN THE CAFÉ

She'd slept in her drywall cocoon on seven, waking three minutes before her alarm, her pulse steady and low. She walked the perimeter, mapped the new dust patterns, and slipped down the service stairwell without being seen. In the gym's locker room, she washed her T-shirt in the sink, used the hand dryer to dry it, braided her hair tightly, and scrubbed the construction grit from the insides of her elbows.

By the time she reached the lobby café, it was still in shadow, all fake woodgrain and quiet glass. She reset the chairs and wiped down the counter as if she could erase the last fingerprints of yesterday. The real morning would start when the Tower's lights blinked on, but she liked these minutes before the suits, before Marcy's voice, before the day's complications.

The café existed in its own microclimate. Ambient music set to barely audible. Pastry shelf backlit. Air always a few degrees colder than the rest of the lobby. The security gate would stay down for another five minutes, but already Mara could see shapes pacing outside: the woman from Legal with her tiny purse and predatory walk, two data guys in matching company hoodies, a new junior staffer with a laptop hugged to his chest.

Marcy arrived at 5:59 a.m., crowing, "You'll not believe what came up last night." The eyeliner from yesterday had migrated into something smudged and exhausted. She didn't even take off her coat. She leaned over the counter and lowered her voice. "Did you hear about the Phantom?"

Mara gave her the blank stare, perfected over years of customer service.

"I'm serious," Marcy said, eyes wide. "Okay, tenth-floor printer, you know, the one that's been dead for months. Someone fixed it overnight a few nights back. It works now. And get this, Security says nobody signed in after 9:30 p.m. But the job log shows two hundred pages printed at 1:41 a.m."

"Maybe it fixed itself," Mara said, without expression.

Marcy snorted. "Or maybe the Phantom did it. Janis says she heard someone moving on three after hours, but when she went to look, nothing. Not even footprints in the wax." She grinned, satisfied. "I love this story."

Mara unlocked the cash drawer, listening. "Did Janis actually see anything?"

"No, but that's the best part." Marcy bounced on her toes. "It's all rumor, so everyone fills in the blanks. By noon, the Phantom will have a backstory. Probably tragic. That's how these things work."

The lights came up in the lobby. Regulars clustered at the gate in a single-file organism hungry for caffeine.

"Should I open early?" Mara asked.

Marcy shrugged, already shrugging out of her coat. "They look like they'll eat the glass if you don't."

Mara lifted the security gate.

Legal Woman led the charge, ordering two macchiatos and a "gluten-free if you have it." The line behind her morphed into conversation.

"You hear about the printer?" Legal said, not even waiting for a reply.

The IT guy next in line said, "My office was hot as hell this morning. Thermostat's fixed, I guess."

"Phantom," Marcy said, like an invocation.

IT guy grinned. "Right. Ghost of the tower. At least it's a compassionate one."

Mara worked the register, careful to look at each customer's face and not at the way the rumor was already mutating.

By 6:12 a.m., the place was alive. Marcy worked the bar, fielding each new Phantom update like a talk show host. She pulled shots, steamed milk, and threw questions into the air. "So what would you do if you caught the Phantom?"

"Does the Phantom get benefits?"

"Is it an actual ghost, or just some Facilities guy with no life?"

A woman from HR joined in, voice pitched high for attention. "You know the package room on five? There's a box that's been there since December. Yesterday it was gone. Security checked the footage. The only person who went in was the cleaning crew. But the sign-out sheet was signed P.H." She tapped her access badge. "Phantom of the Holdings. It's a joke now."

Someone else, junior guy, plaid shirt, maybe finance, said, "I bet it's the same person who keeps fixing the fridges in the break rooms. Sometimes the snacks are restocked, too. No one knows how."

Marcy howled with laughter. "So we're dealing with a snack-obsessed vigilante?"

"It's not a bad system," Mara said quietly, sliding a cup down the bar.

Marcy caught her eye and grinned. "I knew you'd be on Team Phantom."

Mara blinked. "I don't believe in ghosts."

"That's what a ghost would say." Marcy started a new row of cups, labeling each with an exaggerated PH in Sharpie. "We need a Phantom Watch. A sightings board."

She fetched a pad from under the counter, ripped off a sheet, and wrote in giant letters: PHANTOM WATCH. She pinned it to the corkboard where people usually left ads for cat-sitting or old IKEA furniture. "We should track every incident," she declared. "It'll give Security something to do."

Within ten minutes, the board sprouted its first response. A customer scribbled, "Phantom fixed my wobbly chair, thanks!" Another wrote, "The towel dispenser in the eleventh-floor restroom finally works, thank you, Phantom." Someone added a crude stick figure with a question mark for a face.

Marcy took it as her personal mission. She circulated, asking regulars if they'd witnessed any paranormal building maintenance. "Don't be shy," she told an intern, who confessed that her jammed locker had opened on Monday morning. "Classic Phantom move," Marcy said, dead serious.

Mara mostly listened. She kept her head down, but each new story tightened something in her chest. She catalogued every supposed miracle and cross-checked it with what she'd done after hours. Most of it was fantasy, but a few, the printer on ten, the thermostat, the break room fridge, were hers.

Mara thought of her father, the way he used to let her trail him through other people's houses while he worked. He never explained much. He handed her a flashlight and said, "Hold this," or asked her to flip a switch while he listened. She learned the weight of tools, the patience of testing something twice, the habit of putting things back the way you found them. She learned that most problems announced themselves if you stayed still long enough. She hadn't set out to remember any of it. It was just there, waiting.

At 6:34 a.m., a regular who always wore the same moss-colored fleece said, "I thought I saw someone in the garden last night, after midnight. He was sitting on the bench and didn't move for an hour. I only saw him when I went to smoke."

Marcy said, "Spooky," but her eyes flicked to Mara, searching for a reaction.

Mara reached for a milk carton and made herself move slowly. She didn't look up.

The day wore on. By 9:00 a.m., the watch board was full. Doors left mysteriously unlocked. Restocked snacks. A men's room toilet that now flushed without fail.

One of the lawyers returned, holding up her phone, face bright with the thrill of being the first to report something. "There's a thread on Reddit," she said. "It's everywhere. Phantom of the Holdings strikes again."

Marcy cackled. "We're going viral."

Mara smirked. "Careful what you wish for."

"Oh, I want this," Marcy said. "I want the Phantom to become corporate lore. It's all we have left."

Mara tried to picture herself as a ghost. It didn't fit. She was too solid, too tired, too intent on holding to whatever surface she could find. Still, she felt something sharp in watching people latch onto a story that made the day feel less predictable.

Near closing, Marcy added a new line to the board. "Prediction: by Friday, the Phantom will have its own emoji."

Mara looked at the tangle of notes and felt something between pride and dread. Mostly, she felt relief. Nobody was looking at her. They were looking for someone else, someone impossible.

At close, she wiped down the counter, flipped the sign to See You Tomorrow, and paused to read the board one last time. The last note of the day was written in tight, nervous script.

"Phantom, if you're reading this, please fix the lights in the twentieth-floor stairwell. It's scary up there."

Mara tore it off and folded it into her pocket.

As she did, the paper made a small, dry sound. Marcy's head turned at the wrong moment, eyes flicking down to Mara's hand.

Mara held still for half a second too long.

Then she slid the note into her apron as if it were nothing. Just paper. Just trash. Just another thing the café collected.

Marcy stared, almost curious, then shook it off and went back to wiping down the pastry case.

Mara kept her expression flat until her face felt like her own again.

She'd take care of it tonight.

***

The next morning, the lobby café was overrun by 8:20 a.m. Half the building lined up in uneven clumps, everyone talking at once. The air carried perfume and anxiety and the sour note of too much coffee on too little sleep. Mara moved behind the counter with deliberate calm, pulling shots and foaming milk, never once missing a cup or sleeve. Around her, the noise built and built, then crashed against the edges of her focus.

At least three groups were arguing about the Phantom before they reached the register.

"I swear that door was jammed for a week. Now it swings like new," said a guy with earbuds and an access badge that read JUNIOR ANALYST. He wore his lanyard like a medal.

Across the line, someone shot back, "It's Facilities. You think ghosts do work orders?" Laughter followed, then someone from Design said, "I hope the Phantom comes for the copier on thirteen. It's possessed."

Marcy worked the register, playing ringleader. "Anyone seen the Phantom in person? Actual eyes-on?"

An intern, nervous and eager, said, "My friend saw him. A guy in a hoodie cleaning out the break room kitchen at three a.m."

"Legend," Marcy declared, and high-fived him like he just scored a touchdown.

A mid-level manager shook his head, disgusted with the whole building for having a personality. "You people are ridiculous. It's someone running night shift. Or Security pulling a prank."

Marcy grinned. "If it's a prank, they're committed. There's a new sighting every day."

Mara poured drip, slid it down the counter, and kept her face blank. She'd fixed the stairwell light last night, a loose wire and a tired ballast, but the story had already mutated. According to the Watch board, the Phantom had banished the lower stairs and saved a VP from certain doom. The VP in question was in line tapping his phone, oblivious.

Marcy refreshed the thread on her phone. "Update. Someone on six says the Phantom fixed the lock on the bathroom, and now it doesn't rattle at all."

The manager scoffed. "Coincidence. You all want to believe in something, so you invent a ghost."

Marcy nodded, amused. "Or maybe the building finally decided to fix itself."

"Spooky," Mara said, and Marcy laughed.

The copier guy from Facilities showed up looking wrecked. "I need six shots," he said, voice flat.

"Paper jams again?" Mara asked.

He shook his head. "No paper jams. That's the problem. Everything's working. I'm going to be out of a job if this keeps up."

Marcy looked at Mara. "Phantom?"

Mara shrugged. "That, or someone's finally paying attention."

Janis drifted past with her mop cart, eyes scanning for spills and excuses. She smirked at the noise and said, more to herself than anyone else, "Ghosts don't fix anything. If you want something done, you do it."

Marcy beamed. "Janis, are you the Phantom?"

Janis snorted. "If I was, you'd all be out of a job."

A few people laughed, and the laugh held longer than it should have.

Later, as the line ebbed, the skeptical manager returned with two coworkers and a face that said he was already composing an email. He kept his voice low, but Mara caught enough. He wanted the rumors squashed. He said it made the company look unprofessional. One coworker said that it made the place more interesting. The manager ignored her, ordered tea, and left without tipping.

By late morning, the café settled back into its usual pace, but the Phantom didn't. The board was fuller. The thread was faster. People were less careful about who heard them.

Mara watched the myth spread and felt the shift underneath it. The joke had become a building-wide conversation that didn't need permission.

During a lull, Marcy leaned in, voice lower. "You ever wonder if the Phantom knows people are talking about him?"

Mara smiled, just enough to show her teeth. "Maybe that's why he does it."

Marcy nodded, satisfied. "I'd do the same."

A shadow fell across the corkboard. Someone stood there long enough to block the light.

Mara looked up and saw a security guard she didn't recognize. Not Walt. Not one of the sleepy desk guys. This one had a new jacket, a neat badge, and a pen already in hand.

He didn't smile.

He read the notes without touching them, eyes moving faster than a casual glance. Someone had started leaving offerings on the counter for the Phantom: granola bars, a bottle of water with a label marked PHANTOM. Then he looked at Marcy.

"Who started this?" he asked.

Marcy's smile stayed in place out of habit. "It's a corkboard. People write stuff."

The guard looked at Mara next, as if she were part of the furniture and had suddenly decided to speak. "If you hear anything specific," he said, voice even, "times, locations, names, you can report it."

Mara nodded once. "Sure."

The guard remained another second, then walked toward the security desk, posture tight.

Marcy watched him go. Her grin faded.

"Well," she said quietly. "That's new."

Mara wiped the counter once, slowly. "It was always going to become new."

Marcy swallowed and tried to make it a joke again. "Maybe the Phantom will fix Security's attitude."

Mara didn't answer. She could feel the paper in her apron pocket from yesterday, the stairwell note folded down to a hard edge. She could feel the building tightening in places she couldn't see.

At closing, she wiped down the counter and read the board one last time. Someone had added a new note in sharp, hurried writing.

"Phantom, they're watching now."

Mara didn't take that one. She didn't need to.

She zipped her jacket and left through the staff corridor. She didn't head anywhere important yet. It was too early for that.

She took the service stairs up to seven and slipped into her hideout, letting the Tower finish emptying itself. She waited through the after-work drift, the late meetings, the cleaners with their carts and keys.

When the building finally went quiet, when the lobby light dulled, and the noise flattened into machinery and air, Mara pulled the A. Morales access badge from her pocket, ran her thumb over the worn photo, and started her real shift.

Tonight, she was fixing a story that had started to look at her back.

CHAPTER EIGHT

CLEAN SWEEP FOUR

R ick Holman's first hour was always the same. Shoes squeaking on the blue floor. A lap around the GSOC bunker. A signature on the sheet. A scan of the wall of monitors like the building might have changed overnight.

It never changed. It just exposed new mistakes.

At 5:17 a.m., he settled behind the screens labeled Building Integrity: West Campus and pulled up the incident log: ELEVATOR #5: UN-SCHEDULED RUN 0214, NO ACCESS BADGE ON FILE.

"Again," he said, running his thumb over his mustache.

He called up the feed.

Two hours of nothing. Then the freight doors shuddered open on seven, dumped a pair of janitorial carts, and closed for ten seconds. The elevator moved again, empty on camera, drifting down to three. One blurred shape crossed frame, maybe a mop handle, maybe just motion. Then the system reset at 5:00 a.m., as if nothing had happened.

Rick replayed it once.

Twice.

On the third pass, he stopped pretending it was nothing.

A voice from the next desk said, "Someone's joyriding the freight again."

Rick didn't turn. "Manifest."

"Janitorial, by the log. But Janis says she wasn't on that run." Alex leaned in with a vending machine Danish still in plastic, crumbs already threatening the keyboard. "Also, the forums are losing their minds. They think we've got a ghost."

Rick grunted.

Alex flicked a crumb off the desk. "You think it's that Phantom thing?"

Rick side-eyed him. "I think it's someone who knows our gaps. Contractor. Floater. Somebody is using the building as their own."

He pulled the access badge records from 2:00 a.m. to 4:00 a.m. Six swipes, all accounted for. Two Facilities. Three janitorial. One security guard.

His own.

Rick scrolled back and found the gap. 2:14 a.m., elevator movement, no access badge at the reader. No camera hit that showed a person in the elevator.

He zoomed in on the freight doors and watched them close again.

There. A fraction of lag. Not enough to trip an alert. Enough for someone to slip in behind a cart.

Rick pointed at the screen. "See that!"

Alex nodded, impressed. "Nice catch. You want me to escalate?"

"Not yet." Rick leaned back, massaged the bridge of his nose. "If we escalate now, Facilities gives excuses, HR gives emails, and nothing changes. We fix it ourselves."

Alex swallowed the last bite of Danish. "So what, stake it out."

"We run a Clean Sweep." Rick said it like a verdict. "Full rounds every two hours. Staggered routes. Random access badge checks at elevator lobbies and service corridors. No one moves unaccounted for until we find the source."

Alex's eyebrows lifted. "You want me to spin it as a systems test."

Rick's smile was thin. "It is a systems test. Nobody says manhunt. We validate compliance."

He called over Maddy.

Maddy rolled her chair in with her phone still to her ear, expression neutral. She had a way of looking alert even when she wasn't moving. She noticed everything and documented it as a record or complaint.

She ended the call and arched an eyebrow. "Ready for another round, boss."

"Clean Sweep Four," Rick said. "Extra emphasis on mechanicals, stairwells, perimeter doors. Log anomalies. Escalate repeats."

Maddy repeated it word for word into her headset. Rick liked that about her. No performance. Just procedure.

Rick stood and did a slow walk of the GSOC perimeter. Twenty-six feeds on the wall. Four out for scheduled maintenance. Typical.

He keyed the radio. "Status."

Scott's voice came in low. "Floors one through four clear. Loading dock quiet. Want me to run the freight cage?"

"Affirmative," Rick said. "And check the east stairwell."

"Copy."

Rick watched the floor map populate with blue lines as patrols began to move. The building was waking. The net was tightening. He told himself it would hold.

Then he looked at the freight feed again and felt the same irritation settle behind his ribs.

The best patterns didn't break. They adjusted.

That night, the Tower hunted.

***

At midnight, the seventh floor was supposed to be empty.

Mara waited behind the drywall stack, counting time by the faint chime of the glass elevator call bell. Three chimes, then nothing, then three again. Shift change. The building should be quiet.

She rolled off her cardboard mat, limbs heavy from compressed sleep. Tonight's list was small. Fix a jammed faucet in the break room on five. Swap a dying bulb in the copy center on two. In and out. No drama.

She gathered her things, the Morales access badge, a flathead screwdriver left behind by Sammy, and checked the seam in the drywall for light.

A thin glow, not enough to suggest anyone out there.

She zipped her jacket, slid the access badge into her sleeve, and moved.

The main corridor was silent except for the digital hiss of motion sensors waking. Mara padded down the hall and hit the elevator call button.

Nothing.

The panel stayed lit, but the elevator didn't come. She waited a second, then pivoted. The elevator logged floors. Cameras loved elevators. Tonight, she needed stairs.

She took them two at a time until she reached five.

The stairwell door opened with a click that felt wrong. Too easy. Too cooperative.

Mara froze and listened.

Voices.

Two, maybe three. One low and steady. One clipped and bored.

She stepped back, let the door ease shut, and pressed her ear to the metal.

"...three minutes, then we swap," a voice said.

"Copy," another answered. "Sweep starts at the break room."

"East corner. If you see anyone, access badge check. No exceptions."

Mara's stomach tightened. Rick, she thought. Clean Sweep Four.

She waited until the voices moved off, then opened the door again, slow, controlled. She slipped into the hallway, stayed to the blind side, and moved with purpose. Walk like you belong. Don't look like you're listening.

She reached the break room and shut the door behind her.

The lights were off, but the city's glow showed enough to work by. She flipped the faucet lever and confirmed the jam. Stiff. Catching on an internal burr. She crouched, unscrewed the handle, ran the flathead through its seat, and felt a tiny curl of metal shave loose.

It tinked against the sink.

Mara winced, pocketed the evidence, and ran the water once to test.

Fixed. Two minutes.

She wiped the counter, reset the handle, and listened at the door.

Nothing.

She cracked it open and scanned the hallway.

Empty.

Then a flashlight beam swept the far end of the corridor, low and steady, moving like someone with time.

Mara ducked back, closed the door, and crouched by the trash bin. Her heart tried to run ahead of her. She slowed it the way she slowed everything, one breath at a time.

The beam passed. Footsteps followed. A uniformed guard paused outside the break room and checked the handle, like this was the whole point of his life.

Then he moved on.

Mara waited for the echo to die and made a choice.

Only one more fix for tonight.

She slid out and took the west stairwell down toward two, hugging the rail. The air changed as she descended. Cooler. Cleaner. The building's sleeping systems making their own sound.

At two, she opened the stairwell door a hair and checked the corridor.

Freshly mopped. Chemical tang still sharp. The copy center door stood open.

Mara slipped inside.

The room held five copiers, a wall of cabinets, and a bulb that flickered at half intensity. She reached up to twist it free, towel shielding her fingers.

A radio squawked close.

Mara froze with the bulb half turned.

"Copy center clear," a woman's voice said, too near. "You see anything on cams?"

A male voice answered from farther off. "Negative. Everything reads clean. Check mechanical."

The door creaked open.

The officer stepped inside. Tall. Hair shaved at the sides. Badge clipped high. Eyes scanning corners, not people. The kind of look that didn't belong to boredom.

Mara pressed flat against the wall behind the door, breath held, trusting the angle.

The officer made a slow circuit. Hand brushed the top of a copier. Eyes moved to the cabinets.

She opened the supply closet, peered inside, shut it.

Then she left, door still half open behind her.

Mara didn't move for a full minute.

When her lungs finally forced her to breathe, she lowered the towel and left the bulb where it was.

Not worth it.

She slipped out into the service corridor.

At the intersection to the main hall, she paused and listened. Quiet.

She turned the corner and almost collided with a guard.

Older. Stubble. Tired eyes that still caught details.

He glanced at her sleeve where the badge sat, then at her face. "You're Special Projects."

Mara nodded once and forced a tired frown. "Copy center bulb. Got a call."

He didn't question it. He looked past her down the corridor. "Stay safe. There's been some issues tonight."

"Yeah," Mara said. "I heard."

He moved on, but his eyes tracked her a second too long.

Mara didn't run.

She walked three more steps like she belonged there.

Then she darted into the stairwell and took the steps up fast enough to make her knees complain.

On three, she ducked into a janitorial closet. Mop bucket still dripping. She sat on an upturned milk crate and breathed shallow.

Radios barked in the hall. Footsteps overlapped.

"...next round in ten."

"Copy. Stairwells first. They said there's a pattern. Contractor, maybe. Squatter."

Mara stared at the concrete wall and let the words settle.

Squatter.

She wiped her hands on her pants and checked the Morales badge through her sleeve. Still there. Still warm from her skin.

The glue on the back had started to peel.

Mara waited five minutes, then slipped out.

This time she moved like a worker with a task and a route, not like a person trying to vanish. She walked toward a service checkpoint, swung her access badge so it would be seen, and kept her shoulders set.

At the checkpoint, a bored guard looked up from a tiny TV propped on a stack of pallets. He glanced at her access badge and didn't read it long enough to care.

"You're not supposed to be here after two," he said.

"Facilities asked," Mara said, and lifted the access badge as if that were the whole conversation.

He shrugged, lazy with policy. "Go through the north next time. This is deliveries only."

"Okay."

He waved her on.

Mara stepped into the lobby and ducked behind the coffee kiosk where the cameras couldn't see her face straight on. She exhaled hard, then forced her breathing back into a normal rhythm.

She had gotten away with it.

Barely.

The building had changed. The sweeps were tighter. The radios were awake. The patrols moved in pairs.

Mara went back up to seven and slipped into her hiding place behind the drywall stack, heart still thudding.

She stayed there, counting cycles, listening to the building reset itself.

She waited, listening, and realized something that felt like relief and dread at the same time.

The sweeps had a rhythm now, and she could hear it moving past her.

***

At 3:08 a.m., an elevator landed somewhere above her. The bass thump traveled through beams and drywall and shook a little dust loose. Mara waited.

Another elevator stopped two floors down.

Then silence again.

She slid out from behind the drywall and checked the corridor.

Empty.

She moved toward the stairwell and stopped.

A mop cart was parked in the intersection, positioned with care. It blocked the new temporary camera's line of sight by a perfect wedge. Blue towels stacked. Spray bottles lined up. Bucket full.

Janis leaned against the far wall, arms crossed, rag in hand.

Janis raised her eyebrows once, like she was clearing a lane.

Mara stepped into the cart's shadow and pivoted left, slipping past the camera's gaze. As she passed, Janis wrung her rag with slow indifference.

"They just put that up," Janis said, not looking at her. "Be careful."

"Always," Mara replied, voice low enough to be swallowed by the hall.

Mara took the stairs down and cut through mechanical, where pumps and fans made a constant roar that covered footsteps. The air smelled metallic. Condensation glistened on pipes.

At the far end, a maintenance panel sat open, held by a strip of blue tape.

Just enough.

Mara ducked in, elbows and knees scraping, and crawled through a service run that bypassed two cameras and one checkpoint. It emptied into a closet propped open by a toolbox.

Sammy stood inside, hands in his pockets, eyes sharp.

He looked at Mara, then at the open panel behind her. "Didn't think you'd use that."

"You left it for me," Mara said.

Sammy shrugged. "Maybe."

"Clean Sweep," Mara said.

He nodded. "Rick's nervous. He hates patterns he can't break. When he gets nervous, he makes it everyone else's problem."

"You're risking a lot," Mara said.

"So are you," Sammy replied.

They stood in the tight quiet for a second. Then Sammy shifted his weight, like he'd decided what kind of person he was going to be.

"If you keep to mechanical for the next hour, you'll miss two sweeps," he said. "They're focused on lobbies and conference floors."

"Thanks."

Sammy picked up his toolbox. "Nobody checks ducts on sub two. Security hates that level. Too much HVAC noise. Too many places to get turned around."

Mara filed it away.

Sammy left first, walking like he had nothing to hide.

Mara moved through mechanical corridors, hands on cold metal for balance, taking the narrowest passages. She caught the bleach scent of a cleaning crew and stopped before she rounded a corner. She doubled back and took another branch.

When she reached the loading dock stairwell, the reader blinked green.

The bored guard was still in the glass booth, still watching his tiny TV.

Mara swung her access badge in plain sight and walked through like she'd been sent.

He barely glanced up.

She made it back to the lobby, then back to seven, and slipped into her drywall nest as if she'd never moved.

The building was still searching. Radios still barked. Patrols still overlapped.

But the net had holes.

And now she knew which hands were keeping them open.

***

In the GSOC, Maddy watched the floor map update in clean lines and colored dots. Patrols in place. Timers staggered. Nodes covered.

A log entry blinked.

Freight movement at 2:14 a.m. again.

No access badge record.

No camera hit.

A blip that crawled, stalled, then vanished.

Maddy screen-captured it and opened a new incident file. The repetition was the reason.

She printed the screenshot and circled the time with a pen, neat and firm. She placed it on Rick's desk where he couldn't pretend he hadn't seen it.

When Rick arrived, he picked it up and stared.

Maddy's voice stayed flat. "It happened again."

Rick's jaw tightened. "Where?"

"Freight," Maddy said. "Same behavior. Same gap."

Rick looked at the map, then back at the feed, then at the circled time.

"Keep recording," he said.

Maddy nodded. "Already doing it."

Rick held the paper for another second, then set it down like evidence.

He didn't say ghost.

He didn't say Phantom.

He didn't say squatter.

He said the only thing that mattered.

"Pattern."

Mara returned to the seventh floor to lie behind the drywall stack and listened to the building breathe. The sweeps would tighten again. The corridors would change. The net would learn.

She would learn faster.

She closed her eyes and mapped the next move.

CHAPTER NINE

THE WHITE TABLECLOTH GHOST

The opening shift moved slowly, the lobby air bright but not yet awake. Marcy flitted from register to pastry case, recounting the latest Phantom rumor to the few customers in line. They absorbed her voice like caffeine and smiled politely, already halfway inside their next meeting.

Mara kept to the bar, hands on the polished steel, counting down the seconds between each order. She preferred the lull, the way the space stretched and snapped back into shape. The hiding had stopped feeling like a crisis and had become routine; she could run on autopilot.

The first hint of trouble came in the sound of heels.

The catering lead crossed the lobby as if she were late to her own emergency, binder clamped under one arm. Two junior staff followed in parkas, their eyes wide and their faces blank with preemptive dread. The lead's hair was pulled so tight it looked laminated.

Marcy caught her eye and did her "What's the drama" smile. "What do you need today? Two large pots, dark, and the gluten-free box? Need it on the cart?"

The lead looked past Marcy toward the glass corridor, where post-breakfast light raked every surface. "We're staging at eleven. Big white cart. And we need access to the south elevator. Security says it's locked until the sweep. Which is, apparently, now."

"Event on two?" Marcy asked, already at the urns.

"Office suite," the lead replied. "But they want setup by eleven sharp. The GSOC says the entire corridor is on camera for compliance during prep. Full coverage. No loitering in view."

One of the juniors leaned closer, voice lowered. "They flagged our last run because someone left a pallet jack in frame. We had to fill out a report."

Marcy whistled. "A pallet jack. Bold."

The lead shrugged, the gesture of someone who had learned the shrug was the only part of her that still belonged to her. "Policy. Can we get the cart early? The big white one from the dock."

"Give us ten," Marcy said, then turned to Mara. "You wanna pull it? I'll handle the brew."

Mara nodded, grateful for the excuse to leave the counter. She wiped her hands, grabbed the service corridor key, and ducked into the employee hallway.

As she walked, the catering lead's words replayed in her head. Compliance audit. Full coverage. No loitering. The Tower was always watching, but now the watching had teeth.

The service hallway was empty. Mara pushed through the swinging doors toward the catering bay. The smell back here was always the same: bleach and wet cardboard, plus burnt coffee baked into concrete. She found the cart at the end of the row, a white banquet cart with four wheels and a lower shelf lined in non-slip matting. It was built for weight.

It was built for catering, and catering meant loads that could crush toes if you were careless.

Someone had left a stack of clean trays on top, their edges perfect as playing cards. Mara gripped the handle and rocked the cart side to side, testing the wheels. The axle wobbled slightly, stubborn but functional, like a person who had been overworked for years and still showed up anyway.

She rolled it toward the café, then stopped at the swinging door and looked out toward the glass corridor.

In daylight, it was just a hallway with an ego. At night it would be something else. Bright inside, dark outside. A display case.

Full coverage was what Security called it when they wanted people to behave. Full coverage was what they said when they needed the building to believe in them.

Mara steered the cart into the café.

Marcy was already mid-story, inventing a legend on the fly for the catering lead's benefit. "The Phantom only comes out during audits," Marcy said, voice solemn. "White gloves, perfect posture. If you leave a crumb on the tray, he eats your soul."

One of the juniors grinned, nervous more than amused. "We'll be extra careful."

The catering lead checked her watch. "We're supposed to be on site at ten forty-five. Where do you want us until then?"

Marcy gestured toward a table by the window. "Chill here. We'll run your drinks when they're ready. Try not to look guilty."

Mara loaded the gluten-free box onto the cart and stepped aside. The lead tested the lower shelf, pressed down on the handle, nodded approval. "Perfect. We'll wheel it over at the top of the hour."

Mara watched the crew settle in, sipping coffee and half-whispering about the sweep. One of them pulled out a phone and opened what looked like a floor plan, tracing a path through the glass corridor and tapping at tiny camera icons like they were landmines.

Mara drifted to the edge of the café and checked the lobby clock. Ten minutes. Enough.

She wiped down the counter once, then slipped out the side door and looped toward the corridor's far end.

The light was harsher here, high-watt LEDs spaced so the glass showed every fingerprint and smudge. Mara walked the length slowly, pretending to study fire extinguisher mounts. What she really studied were angles. Exposure. Reflection.

The corridor cameras were mounted high and aimed down the run, good for faces and lanyards and people who walked like they had somewhere important to be. They were less interested in equipment that moved through the building all day. Carts. Mop rigs. Trays. Things Security couldn't afford to flag constantly without drowning in their own alerts.

A cart moving down this corridor at night would look normal on paper. The question was whether the system could be made to see only the cart.

Mara stopped at the midpoint and looked out through the glass. The sidewalk was visible, a strip of city that didn't belong to the Tower. People passed with their heads down, phones in their hands. Later, there would be smokers and rideshare waits and bored strangers with nothing to do but stare at bright things.

She pictured the corridor after midnight, glowing white and blue. She pictured a white shape drifting through it. She pictured the GSOC operator leaning forward, squinting, trying to decide whether the building was broken or they were.

It was the feeling of finding a seam in something that claimed it had no seams.

When Mara returned to the café, the morning had restarted at full volume. The catering lead was waiting at the bar, coffee in one hand, pen tapping the counter.

"You want to watch us run the corridor?" she asked, half-joking.

Mara kept her face blank. "I'll catch it later."

The lead laughed and wheeled the cart toward the glass corridor, her crew trailing behind. Mara watched the white cart float across the lobby. She watched the camera's cold black eye follow it without emotion. She memorized the pace. She memorized how the cart's bright plastic looked under those LEDs, how the glass turned edges soft.

By the time the catering crew disappeared around the corner, the plan in Mara's head had crossed over into a dare.

***

By closing, the idea had sharpened into something almost clean. Mara didn't tell Marcy. Mara didn't tell anyone. The Tower was full of people who loved to talk. Mara had survived twenty years by knowing when to keep her mouth shut.

That night, after the last customer left and the café gate rolled down, Mara moved through her routine with a steadier hand than usual. She cleaned. She counted. She locked up. She let her body pretend it was going to sleep.

But her mind stayed awake, building a corridor out of light.

Clean Sweep Four had changed the Tower's rhythm. More radios. More footsteps that meant something. More doors opening and closing with intent. Mara waited in the places she knew were safe, listening for the cadence of patrol shoes and the silence that followed them.

When the building finally went quiet enough to move, the clock in the service corridor read 2:34 a.m.

Mara slipped toward the lobby elbow where the white banquet cart waited. Someone had draped a white tablecloth over the top deck after the catering run, the linen hanging loose like an afterthought.

Mara tugged the cloth down until it fell past the axle. She adjusted the hem lower, then lower again, until it grazed the tile. The cloth would hide wheels. It would hide shoes. It would hide anything that depended on the floor for proof of life.

The cart was built for weight. It could carry stacks of plates, full chafers, entire meals for people who never learned the names of the workers who fed them.

It could carry her.

Mara climbed onto the lower shelf and sat with her knees tucked, feet pulled up so nothing touched the tile. She slid her hands under the frame and hooked her fingers around a crossbar just behind the wheel housing. From the outside, there would be no hands. No feet. No walking. Only a white drape and a moving bulk.

She took one breath and pulled with her hands.

The cart rolled forward, quiet at first, then louder as it crossed the first seam in the tile. Mara kept the motion steady. She used momentum, tugging in small controlled movements so the cart glided between pulls. A consistent pace was the lie. A consistent pace said object, object, object.

When she reached the glass corridor, the light changed. White and blue. Cold and clinical. LEDs hit the linen and the fabric bloomed bright, edges softened by glare. The corridor reflected itself back into infinity. A white shape in a mirrored hallway looked like an error.

Mara kept herself low. She kept her head down. She didn't let her shoulders rise above the line where the cloth hung. If the system saw anything, she wanted it to see only bright fabric and drift.

Halfway through, the wheels caught on a raised seam and the cart stalled.

Mara froze with it.

A radio chirped somewhere close enough that she felt it in her chest.

"...north glass corridor, check the cart staging. Sweep still on..."

The voice was half swallowed by static, but the words were clear enough.

Someone was awake.

Mara didn't move. She didn't breathe deeply. She let the cart sit as if it belonged there, as if it had always been there.

Footsteps clicked on tile somewhere beyond the glass. Just passing, the way guards passed when they weren't interested.

Mara counted to ten, then shifted her weight and let the cart rock once, barely a wobble.

It felt ridiculous. It felt childish. It felt perfect.

From the outside, it would look like the ghost had adjusted itself.

Mara pulled again. The wheels bumped over the seam. The cart continued, smooth as before.

Through a narrow gap near the hem, she saw the sidewalk beyond the glass. Two figures had stopped outside, faces turned upward toward the bright corridor. One lifted a phone. A rectangle of light appeared, then another. Mara couldn't see their expressions, but she could imagine them. Confusion first. Then delight. Then the reflex to document, because no one believed anything that wasn't recorded.

Mara kept moving, and for the first time in a long time, she felt something that was almost pleasurable. She had made the watchers look foolish without saying a word.

Near the far end, she guided the cart into the service alcove where reflections thinned. She stopped it beside the dumbwaiter and waited until her pulse slowed.

Then she slid off the shelf into the recess without lifting the cloth and slipped through the service door into a narrow storage space lined with old chairs. She shut the door without letting it click.

Inside, the silence was total. Her ears rang with her own blood. She leaned both hands against the wall and breathed until the adrenaline burned itself down.

She had done it.

A systems exploit dressed in linen.

Outside, the phones stayed raised. Someone laughed, a quick surprised sound, then said something that didn't carry through the glass. The other person kept filming.

The clip went up online before anyone inside the Tower admitted it had happened.

It hit the building thread first. A shaky video, reflections multiplying the white blur until it looked like it floated. The caption was short, dumb, and confident.

"The Phantom spotted. I swear," read the post along with a ten-second video.

Within minutes, the comments split into predictable camps. Catering cart. Performance art. Real ghost. Inside job. Someone demanded time stamps. Someone else posted a screen grab and said the building was falling apart.

By 3:14 a.m., it reached Maddy.

***

Maddy wasn't on shift yet. Maddy didn't need to be. She woke early and stayed awake, the way some people stayed armed.

She watched the clip once.

Then again.

Then paused on a frame where the white blur seemed to hover.

Maddy didn't laugh. She didn't roll her eyes. She didn't forward it with a caption.

In Maddy's world, official meant documented. Evidence. A paper trail that could be forwarded, filed, and used later when someone needed a name attached to a mistake. She didn't send the link. Links could be denied. Links could disappear.

Printouts stayed.

She arrived at the GSOC early with coffee in one hand and her phone in the other. The printer whined and spat pages out crooked. Maddy straightened them anyway, precise and patient, like she enjoyed the ritual. Four screenshots per page. Each blur circled in firm red ink.

Alex glanced over from the next desk and blinked. "Is that from Reddit?"

Maddy set the pages down like exhibits. "It was filmed outside," she said. "Which means it's our problem inside. We need it on file."

Alex laughed once, sharply. "You printed a haunting?"

"I printed something we'll be asked about," Maddy said, and took a sip of coffee like the matter was settled.

They pulled up the corridor feed. The camera showed exactly what Mara had hoped it would show. A bright flare moving through a bright glass hallway. Edges softened by glare. Reflections multiplying the shape.

The motion system tagged it as unscheduled equipment movement and moved on. No access badge swipe. No face. No lanyard.

Alex scrubbed the timeline and shook his head. "That's a cart wearing linen."

Maddy tapped the paper. "It's also on the internet."

Alex leaned back, amused. "So now it's real."

"Now it's a problem," Maddy said.

When Rick arrived, Maddy was waiting with the printouts on his desk, placed dead center so he couldn't pretend he hadn't seen them.

Rick looked down, then up at her. "Why is this on my desk?"

Maddy's expression stayed neutral. "Because everyone's already talking about it."

Rick picked up a page, stared at the circled blur, then turned toward the monitors. "Show me the feed."

Maddy did. Alex replayed the clip at half speed. The white shape drifted through frame, stalled at the seam, then continued as if it had decided to keep going. Slowed down, it looked worse. Like a thing without weight.

Rick watched without speaking.

"It makes us look stupid," Maddy said, quietly, like she'd found the real offense.

Rick's mouth tightened. "We don't know what it is yet."

Alex said, "We know exactly what it is. It's a cart. It's a cart that has decided it's a ghost."

Rick shot him a look and returned to the screen. "Run a crosscheck. Every corridor camera. Last three nights. Tag anything that moves where it shouldn't."

Maddy's eyes didn't soften. "Already doing it."

Rick held the printed page a second longer, then set it down. "And stop printing things from social media."

Maddy met his eyes, flat and fearless. "It's already printed, sir."

Rick exhaled through his nose. Maddy's tone didn't change, but her intent did. She slid one more page forward, the clearest screen grab, the most humiliating one.

"This will be in the morning briefing," she said. "If we don't have an answer, we'll be the answer."

She said it like a threat, and it was.

CHAPTER TEN

THE GSOC INFILTRATION

Mornings were always carnivorous, but today the café had teeth. The line curled twice around the pillars and stretched toward the lobby's frosted glass, a living diagram of caffeine demand. Marcy worked the register like she was fending off a riot, firing jokes and "next" at a parade of half-zombies in tailored wool. Mara stayed on the bar, pulling doubles with both hands, setting out lids and sleeves, watching the syrup pumps take their daily beating.

She barely noticed the first order slip. The second came with a hard clack, then a third in quick succession. When she finally looked, the new ticket wasn't a drink at all.

SECURITY OPS | GSOC URGENT

4x 96oz Dark Roast

2x 96oz Decaf 6x

Assorted Pastries

Deliver to GSOC by 0800

Mara read it twice, as if the words might change out of embarrassment.

"Basement," she said.

Marcy leaned over the printer, squinted, then made a face that tried to be casual and failed. "They're not allowed windows."

Mara glanced at her.

Marcy shrugged, as if this was common knowledge and not a rumor she had just invented. "Too many secrets. One time, a guy came up here for a latte and spent the whole wait staring at the fire alarms. Like, buddy, relax. It isn't your fault if the building catches on fire."

Mara prepped the pastry box, picking the crumbliest scones. It felt petty. It felt deserved. She checked the time. 7:12 a.m. More than enough buffer if she moved fast.

The basement wasn't her territory. She had never gone lower than the gym. The loading dock was as far down as her life usually went, and she liked it that way. But a job was a job, and the ticket had that particular tone that meant somebody had decided urgency was a personality.

"Want me to run it?" Mara asked, hoping for a yes.

Marcy shook her head, already pulling a shot. "I'm pinned to the machine. You go. They tip weird down there."

That wasn't comforting.

The urns finished within a minute of each other. Mara built the load like she was packing for a short trip: two cardboard caddies labeled with masking tape, the pastry box, napkins, sugar packets, stir sticks, and creamer. The tray weighed more than she expected. She steadied it, wiped her hands, and grabbed the pre-printed receipt Marcy slid across the counter.

"If you get interrogated," Marcy said, "tell them I said hi."

"I sure will," Mara said, and kept her voice dry enough to pass as calm.

She skirted the counter, slipped through the employee hallway, and headed for the staff elevator. The lobby noise fell away behind her, replaced by the hush of back corridors and the particular smell of a building that never fully aired out. Bleach, old coffee, warm dust. The Tower's idea of cleanliness.

The employee elevator took her down in silence. No music. No cheerful voice announcing floors. Just the steady buzz and the faint lurch of cables doing their work.

When the doors opened, the air changed. Cooler. Flatter. Like the building had run out of patience for oxygen. The hallway was wider than the ones above, lined with beige cinderblock and bright fluorescence that made even neutral colors feel hostile. No windows. No plants. No posters pretending to care.

At the end of the corridor stood a steel door and an access badge reader glowing steady red. In this building, red meant no, even before you asked.

Mara adjusted her grip on the tray and told herself she wasn't doing anything wrong. She was delivering coffee. People delivered coffee every day.

She thumbed her access badge.

The light flashed yellow, as if the reader had to think about her, then turned green. The door unlocked with a heavy thunk.

A chair scraped inside the room beyond, the sound sharp through the glass.

Mara kept her face neutral and stepped forward anyway, because hesitation was how you got remembered.

On the other side was a shorter hall with carpet that tried and failed to soften the place. It ended in a glass partition. Behind it, three people in navy polos sat at a horseshoe desk, faces lit by dozens of monitors. The room was windowless except for a one-way mirror that faced back toward her like an accusation.

The space smelled like burnt electronics.

A tall man stood as she approached, broad at the shoulders, mustache trimmed with military precision. He looked like he had been built out of policy.

"Delivery?" he asked.

"Yes."

He pressed a button, and a section of glass slid open just enough to make the room feel like a trap. He didn't look up. "Set it on the table."

Mara carried the tray in and placed it carefully on the cleared corner of a side table. A stack of paper cups sat nearby, untouched. They had the same logo as the ones upstairs, which meant the Tower had managed to brand even the underground.

The mustached man checked the receipt, took the pen clipped to the clipboard, and signed his name with quick certainty. Then he tore off the top copy and slid it across the table toward her, eyes still on the monitors.

A signature. Proof the coffee arrived. Proof that someone down here still believed in paper.

"Thanks," he said, already on a different task.

Mara should have left.

Instead, she stayed.

It was hard not to look. The wall of screens was a grid of the Tower's insides: stairwells, lobbies, hallways, empty conference rooms, elevators opening and closing on nobody. Watching it was like watching the building breathe.

One monitor near the far end played a clip on loop. Bright corridor. White blur drifting through it. Glare and reflection making the shape look like it hovered. The White Tablecloth Ghost, replayed until it became ritual.

Mara felt something lift in her chest. Pride, sharp and stupid. She let it sit there anyway.

The operator running the loop was young and clean-cut, the kind of face that had never been ignored in a room. He had the video slowed down, scrubbing back and forth like he could find the truth by annoying the same ten seconds.

Beside him, a woman with a headset pushed her coffee aside and leaned closer to the screen. She wore a half-smile that said she wanted the clip to be real, if only because it made the shift less dead.

"It doesn't even look like a cart," the woman said.

"It's a cart," the young man snapped back, like he was reciting a script. "It has to be. It just doesn't look like one."

Mara cleared her throat.

Nobody looked at her.

She tried again, louder, as if she belonged here. "Do you really watch all of these at once?"

The woman with the headset finally glanced over, startled, as if she had forgotten service workers could form words. "What?"

Mara nodded at the screens. "All of them. All the time."

The woman laughed once, short and exhausted. "No. The system watches most of it. We watch what screams."

Mara thought about that. She could feel her own boldness like a hand on her back, pushing her forward.

She'd learned where the cameras didn't care. Now she wanted to learn where they did.

"What counts as screaming?" Mara asked.

The young man perked up. He liked this part. He pointed at his monitor as if he were proud of it. "Motion flags. Loitering. Unscheduled equipment movement. Door forced. Access badge mismatch. Stuff like that."

The mustached man's voice carried from his desk without him turning. "And anything that turns into a report."

Mara's gaze drifted back to the loop. "So, the ghost is a report."

The headset woman's smile widened. "The ghost is a headache. Also, the most entertaining thing we've seen in months."

The young man leaned forward. "It started on Reddit."

Mara kept her face blank. "Of course it did."

She set the empty caddies down, just to have something to do with her hands. The questions came easier now, like she had already crossed the line and wanted to see how far it went.

"If the system flags loitering," she said, "how long is loitering?"

The young man answered too quickly. "Depends on the zone. Most places it's two minutes."

"Two," Mara repeated.

"Less if it's after hours," the mustached man said, not looking up. "Less near stairwells. Less near executive corridors."

Mara nodded, filing it away.

"So, carts get flagged," she asked, "or not."

The young man's mouth twisted. "Carts are tricky. The system hates false positives. If we flagged every mop bucket, we'd do nothing else."

The headset woman added, "Carts get forgiveness. People with carts get less. The system can't always tell the difference, so it shrugs, and we decide whether it matters."

Mara looked back at the ghost clip. "And this mattered?"

"It mattered because it's embarrassing," the woman said, matter-of-factly. "And because now everybody thinks they can be creative."

Mara let her eyebrows lift. "Creative how?"

The young man shrugged. "People want something to point at that isn't their job."

Mara glanced at a different screen where a stairwell door sat perfectly still. "So what do you do when something screams?"

The young man brightened again. "You verify. Pull camera. Check access badge logs. Cross-check other cameras. If it repeats, you log it."

"And what makes it a report?" Mara asked.

That question hung longer than the others.

The mustached man glanced over, eyes tired but alert. "Repeat anomalies. Patterned anomalies. Anything that hits the morning briefing. Anything Audit can ask about."

"Audit?" Mara repeated, tasting the word.

The headset woman groaned. "Audit is a personality disorder."

The young man said, "Audit is why we're all here."

Mara nodded, sympathetic, like she had just joined their club.

She should have left then.

Instead, she let herself look around the room one more time.

The headset woman pointed with her coffee cup toward a corkboard above the recycling bin. "Maddy made printouts."

Mara followed the gesture.

Pages pinned crookedly. Four screenshots to a sheet. Each blur circled in red pen. The circles were neat and firm, like someone was grading footage.

Next to the screenshots was an old access badge photo in a cracked plastic sleeve with TERMINATED stamped across it in block letters.

MORALES.

Mara's stomach tightened.

The face wasn't hers, but it could have been. Dark hair pulled back. Controlled mouth. Eyes set the way you learned to set them when you didn't want anyone to ask questions.

Her hand went to her apron pocket before she could stop it.

The Morales access badge was there, flat and warm against her fingers. The adhesive on the back had started to peel. The edge of plastic felt sharp, as if the name could cut her through fabric.

She let her hand fall away. She kept her face blank. She kept her shoulders where they were.

"Who's Maddy?" Mara asked, keeping her voice light.

The young man made a face. "You don't want Maddy to notice you."

The mustached man didn't look up. "Maddy notices everything. Reports everything."

Mara's mouth almost formed a reply.

A chair rolled softly behind her.

Maddy.

Small. Neat. Wide awake. Sweatshirt a size too big. Coffee more cream than coffee. Expression set in that particular blend of concern and satisfaction that came from having spotted a problem before anyone else.

She looked at Mara, then at the tray, then at the corkboard, like the three things formed a narrative she could control if she kept her grip tight enough.

"You're from the café," Maddy said, the way someone reads off a clipboard.

Mara nodded. "Yes."

Maddy's eyes flicked to the ghost printouts, then back to Mara. "Have people been talking about it upstairs?"

"They have phones," Mara said mildly. "They have time. They talk."

Maddy nodded like she had expected exactly that. "It's escalating."

The mustached man said, "Everything escalates if you feed it."

Maddy ignored him. "If you hear specifics, you report them."

Mara blinked slowly. "Like what?"

"Times," Maddy said. "Locations. Direction. Who was nearby. Whether anyone claims they saw it in person. People exaggerate. Patterns don't."

Mara nodded like she was being trained, which she was.

Maddy stepped closer and angled herself just enough that Mara could see a small lens in the corner above the glass. A camera. Active. Watching the doorway.

"Stand right there," Maddy said.

Mara didn't move at first.

Maddy smiled without warmth. "If you're going to loiter in my office, you can do it where the footage is clear."

Mara stepped into the spot.

The headset woman looked down at her console, suddenly very interested in her coffee.

The young man stopped smiling.

Maddy looked at Mara like she was solving a puzzle. "What's your name?"

"Mara," she said.

Maddy didn't write it down. "Last?"

"Flores."

Maddy nodded once, then held out her hand. "Badge."

Mara's pulse jumped, quick and sharp.

"My access badge?" she repeated, like she hadn't heard.

Maddy's voice stayed calm. "Your badge number. Read it off."

Mara swallowed. "R108327."

Maddy repeated it softly, then wrote it on a small yellow sticky note and pressed it to the corner of her monitor, as it belonged there.

It was a small act.

It felt like a bruise.

Mara kept her face neutral. "Do you want the receipt?"

Maddy didn't look at the clipboard. "We have the receipt."

Mara felt the room tilt in a way no elevator ever had.

Maddy's eyes moved over Mara's face again, slow, satisfied. "You ask a lot of specific questions for a barista."

The words hit before she could brace.

Mara let the fear move through her without touching her face. "A lot of people work here."

Maddy held the stare for another second, then looked away as if deciding the feeling wasn't worth paperwork.

"If you hear anything upstairs," Maddy said, "you can tell us."

Mara nodded. "Sure."

"And tell Marcy to stop calling it the White Tablecloth Ghost," Maddy added, flat. "It's inaccurate."

Mara paused, just enough. "What's accurate?"

Maddy said it without irony. "Unidentified after-hours equipment movement."

The headset woman snorted into her coffee.

Maddy didn't blink. "If you want to be helpful, be accurate."

Mara's mouth twitched. She kept it down.

She gathered the used cups, sugar wrappers, and stir sticks, small evidence of a room that tried to erase itself every day. She moved toward the exit at a steady pace.

Behind her, Maddy spoke again, quiet enough to be for Mara alone.

"Oh," she said. "One more thing."

Mara stopped.

Maddy's voice stayed sweet and sharp. "If you come down here again, don't pretend you're curious. Pretend you have permission."

Mara turned slightly. "Do I look like I have permission?"

Maddy's smile widened, thin. "You look like you have questions."

Mara walked out without hurrying. She kept her shoulders loose and her face neutral, like she belonged anywhere a coffee tray belonged.

The hall outside felt louder than before, even though it was still silent. Her footsteps echoed. The elevator ride up felt longer, as if the Tower had decided she needed more time to think about what she had seen.

When the doors opened on the café level, the lobby noise rushed back in. Steam. Voices. Orders. The normal chaos of being visible.

Marcy glanced up as Mara came around the corner. "Well."

Mara set the clipboard down, wiped her hands, and kept her face calm. "They really aren't allowed windows."

Marcy grinned like she'd won something. "See. Secrets."

Mara hesitated, then reached into her apron pocket and pulled out something small and heavy.

A coin.

One of the GSOC operators must have slipped it into her apron while she gathered trash, casual as a tip, the kind of weird gratitude Marcy had promised. It was stamped with SECURITY OPERATIONS on one side and the Tower's logo on the other.

Mara set it on the counter.

Marcy's eyes widened. "No!"

Mara nodded once. "You're right, they do tip weird down there."

Marcy picked it up, turned it over, reverent. "This is funny."

A short laugh slipped out of Mara before she could stop it. It surprised her, and Marcy too. It felt unfamiliar in her throat, like a door she hadn't opened in years.

Mara went back to the bar and started wiping down the steel, but her mind stayed in the basement, in the glow of monitors and the neat red circles on a corkboard.

She had wanted to disappear.

Now Maddy had her badge number on a sticky note.

Maddy thought she was tightening the net.

Mara wiped the counter once more, slow and careful, until her breathing sounded normal again.

Then she kept working, because that was what she did.

CHAPTER ELEVEN

GOING UP

The next morning, by the time the café hit its post-rush lull, Mara's mind was still underground, stuck on a cracked access badge photo and the word TERMINATED stamped across it. The image surfaced at stupid moments. While she rinsed pitchers. While she wiped counters. While she pretended to listen to Marcy narrate the legend of a tablecloth ghost, as if it were a weather report.

She slept badly after the GSOC run. The new shape of the building stuck in her head. The way the GSOC spoke in zones and nodes, in flags and patterns, as if the Tower weren't a place but a system that occasionally swallowed people whole. The way Rick Holman's name sat in their mouths like a rule that didn't need to be written down.

In the café, Marcy was in rare form, crowd-working the lull with fresh embellishments. She had taped another drawing to the Phantom Watch board. A ghost in an apron pushing a cart, a lanyard swirling like a cape. The ghost had eyelashes. The cart sparkled.

Mara let herself drift, hands on autopilot. Rinse. Wipe. Restock. Smile. Next.

When the lobby reset to background noise, she turned toward the glass elevators.

There were two elevator banks.

One was quiet in a way that felt intentional. No scuffed trim. No taped signs. The call panel looked untouched, like the building had installed it for show and then punished anyone who tried to use it. The people who rode those elevators wore matte-black access badges and thick lanyards that lay flat, never flipping, never snagging. Their clothes were pressed with the confidence of dry cleaning billed to someone else.

The other bank was loud, impatient, and always a little late. A printed sign at eye level read: NO PUBLIC ACCESS ABOVE 16. The paper had been replaced more than once, which meant the rule had been tested.

Mara watched a cluster approach the quiet bank. Two men and a woman in navy and oxblood, moving with the floaty arrogance of people who hadn't waited for a crosswalk in a decade. One of the men checked his phone like the air might be emailing him.

The elevator arrived instantly, as if it had been waiting.

Marcy sidled up beside Mara with a milk pitcher and a grin. "I'd kill for those shoes. Actually, I'd kill for the bone structure to survive those shoes."

Mara didn't respond. The doors closed and the three suits vanished into the gold-lit core of the building.

For a second, Mara saw herself reflected in the elevator glass. Rolled sleeves. Wrinkled apron. Her own access badge hanging limp, white lanyard twisted like it couldn't stand itself.

Marcy leaned on the counter. "You ever wonder what floor we'd be on if we were important?"

"I'm content with ground level," Mara said.

"That's what someone stuck on ground level would say." Marcy's grin softened. "Bet they have a better break room up there. Real snacks. Like fruit that isn't decorative."

"The higher you go, the more they feed you," Mara said.

Another group arrived. Access badges aligned. Shoes shined. Voices low enough to be private. They hovered in formation, then stepped into the elevator without ever looking at one another's credentials.

Mara didn't stare. She didn't need to. She filed details away. Who swiped first. How long the doors stayed open. The way the security desk never looked up unless someone made a problem.

Marcy's voice dropped, playful but edged. "I'm telling you. If you wore a suit and didn't talk to anyone, you could get to the penthouse. Just walk in and start ordering people around."

Mara kept her eyes on the elevator bank. "Maybe I will."

Marcy watched her a second longer than usual. "You good?"

"Just tired," Mara said.

"You look like you saw a ghost in the GSOC," Marcy joked.

Mara didn't reply. Mara thought of the corkboard above the recycling bin. Morales. TERMINATED. The stamp was so clean it felt official. The kind of clean that meant erasure.

Mara looked down at her own lanyard, then back at the quiet bank.

If she wanted to cross the border, she didn't need permission. She needed a costume and momentum. That was all.

***

By two o'clock, the café was closed, the gate down, the lobby thinned to meetings and echoes. They cleaned the counter twice. Counted the till.

Locked the drawer. The work ended the way it always did, like it had never mattered.

Marcy slung her bag over her shoulder and stretched. "I'm going home to lie down and stare at the ceiling."

"Sounds right," Mara said.

Marcy glanced at the Phantom Watch board and shook her head. "If that thing asks for a loyalty card, I'm quitting."

Then she was gone, footsteps fading toward the exit.

Mara waited a full minute. Long enough for the lobby to forget her. Long enough for the building's attention to drift upstairs.

She clocked out and walked the employee corridor the way she always did at the end of a shift. Head down. Pace steady. Nothing to see here.

At the junction, she turned left instead of right.

Anyone watching would assume she was heading home. That was the point.

***

The gym door sat where it always had, glass smudged with fingerprints and optimism. A friendly sign listed hours and rules in corporate language.

Mara had passed it a dozen times without slowing down.

She slowed down now.

She lifted the Morales badge to the reader.

The scanner chirped. The lock disengaged.

The system remembered Morales better than it remembered her.

Inside, the gym was nothing special. Treadmills lined up like threats. Free weights. A TV tuned to sports with the sound off. The air smelled like disinfectant and something faintly rotten where the drains met the tile.

The women's locker room was empty except for a cleaner in blue scrubs, mopping around benches with her attention fixed on the floor. The cleaner glanced up when Mara entered, took a look at her access badge at her chest, then looked away.

No suspicion. No recognition. Just another body in the building.

Mara crossed to the lockers. Assigned ones with printed labels. Public ones with cheap combination locks. A lost-and-found bin pushed against the far wall, overflowing with the evidence of other people's intentions.

She dug through it quickly. A marathon sweatshirt. A lone dress shoe. Two blazers, one gray and one black. The black one still held its shape. An access badge sleeve with a broken clip.

She took the blazer, a white blouse with plastic still on the collar, and a pair of dark slacks that looked close enough.

In a bathroom stall, she stripped the café uniform away. Pants. Blouse. Blazer.

The slacks fit at the waist and hung at the ankles. She rolled them once and left it. The blazer fit, as it had belonged to someone who never reached for anything above her head.

She slid the Morales access badge into the black sleeve. The name disappeared. The plastic became anonymous and expensive-looking.

She tied her hair tighter and studied herself in the mirror.

The act wasn't perfect. It didn't need to be.

She stepped out, washed her hands as she belonged there, and found the cleaner still working, now on her knees by the sinks. The cleaner looked up, saw the blazer and access badge sleeve, and returned to her work.

Mara stared at her reflection again. Tall enough. Hair neat. Jacket crisp. The access badge placed where it mattered.

She was nobody.

She was everyone.

She walked out of the gym with a steady, medium-slow pace and headed back toward the lobby. At the newsstand, she looped once, then angled toward the executive elevator bank.

The quiet bank was empty.

Good.

She lifted the access badge to the reader.

The panel blinked. The doors opened.

The elevator was empty, gold-lit, silent. Mara stepped inside and stood as if she had done this her whole life. She randomly pressed 36.

The elevator rose with a smoothness that made the other banks feel like punishment. The vibration barely there.

Mara watched her reflection in the brushed metal. In the blazer, she looked like someone's assistant. Someone's analyst. Someone's problem.

The resemblance hit again. The Morales photo. The same pulled-back hair. The same controlled mouth.

She forced her gaze away.

The numbers climbed.

At twenty-five, the elevator slowed and stopped.

The doors opened onto an executive sky-lobby. Thick carpet. Real plants in soil. Lighting that made everyone look like they slept. The air smelled like lemon polish and money.

Rick Holman stepped in.

He didn't hesitate. He didn't look around. He belonged everywhere the elevator went.

The doors closed.

The elevator resumed its climb.

Rick's gaze flicked to her reflection in the polished metal wall. He took in the blazer, the access badge sleeve, the posture. Something in his eyes caught, just slightly.

He cleared his throat. "You hear about the Phantom?"

"Hard not to," Mara said, with a small laugh.

Rick nodded. "We'll catch him."

Mara turned her head just enough to meet his eyes. "Everyone's heard of her."

The word "her" slipped out clean.

Mara felt it instantly, a small click in her chest. She kept her mouth still. She kept her breathing even. She didn't try to correct it. She didn't try to soften it.

Rick's gaze sharpened.

Mara added smoothly, "The Phantom. It's all anyone talks about."

Rick studied her for another second, then looked away. "I always catch my target."

Mara nodded once, respectful. "That's comforting."

The elevator slowed.

The doors opened onto thirty-six.

Mara stepped out without hurry.

Rick stayed inside, watching her cross the threshold. Watching the access badge sleeve swing once and settle.

At the corner of the corridor, Mara glanced back.

Rick was still looking at her.

She gave him the faintest smile and said, very quietly, "You just missed her."

Then she turned the corner.

Rick lunged forward, hand rising toward the doors. The panels slid shut anyway, smooth and final.

"Son of a bitch!" Rick yelled.

The elevator continued upward.

Rick stood alone in the rising elevator, eyes fixed on his own reflection. No alert. No access anomaly. No report. Just a slip of language and a face that fit too neatly into a pattern. He replayed the moment the way he replayed footage, not as emotion, as data.

Her. Not him.

And the face tugged up an old printout Maddy had pinned to the GSOC wall, stamped in block letters: MORALES. TERMINATED.

He didn't need a confession. He needed one stable detail.

He pulled his phone and made a note with one thumb, fast and quiet.

Phantom likely female. Check recent access badge anomalies. Morales file.

For now, that was enough. The building would give her back to him when it was ready.

***

On thirty-six, Mara walked without looking back. The air tasted like polish and stillness. Framed words about progress and innovation lined the walls, each one expensive enough to be meaningless.

A woman stood near a lounge entrance clutching notebooks. "Are you here for the Heller meeting?" she asked.

"Yes," Mara said.

"Good," the woman said. "Conf 36A. I'm Grace."

Grace held out her hand.

"Morgan," Mara said, taking it.

They walked together down the corridor. A man waved them into a conference room without looking up.

The room was already half-full. People hovered around a long table, opening laptops, aligning water bottles, and straightening nameplates as if hoping for order. The chairs were leather and forgiving. The air conditioning was set to a temperature that assumed nobody had to move for work.

Mara picked a seat near the far end and set her hands on the tabletop.

They were steady.

Then, a second later, she felt the delayed tremor in her fingers, small and private. Something closer to the aftermath of having pushed too hard and gotten away with it.

She curled her hand once under the table and forced it still.

No one questioned her presence.

No one cared.

Grace clicked her pen. "Let's get started."

A man in a blue suit cleared his throat and began speaking in a language made of milestones, intake, and alignment. The words flowed over Mara like elevator music.

Mara nodded at the right moments. She wrote notes on the notepad in front of her. When someone looked her way, she offered a practiced smile. They accepted it and forgot her.

They were all so ordinary. More tired than she'd expected. Some younger than her, wearing exhaustion like a badge.

Halfway through the meeting, the woman beside Mara leaned in and whispered, "First one?"

Mara nodded.

"They're all the same," the woman whispered. "They'll forget what they decided by Friday."

Mara kept her smile small. "I'll keep notes."

The woman's mouth twitched. "We should all do that."

The meeting churned forward. Soft disagreements. Corrections dressed as questions. A hierarchy invisible until you listened for it.

Then, during a lull, a man at the far end turned and looked directly at Mara, like he had finally decided to inventory the room.

His expression was polite, almost relieved.

"You're Morales's replacement, right?" he asked. "Operations. You look just like her."

Mara felt the blood drain from her face.

She kept her posture still. She made her pen move once across the page, a meaningless line that proved her hand still worked.

"Just trying to keep up," Mara said.

The man smiled, satisfied by any answer at all. "Glad to have you. Morales always sat there." He nodded toward the far end of the table like he was pointing out a reserved seat. "Welcome to the show."

As the meeting broke apart, Grace slid a thin stack of handouts down the table. Agenda, timelines, a single page of acronyms nobody bothered to explain. Mara took a copy without comment and tucked it into her blazer pocket with the same care she used for receipts.

No one noticed. Everyone was already late for something else.

Mara stood when they stood. She drifted with the current toward the door, shoulders loose, pace steady. She watched the access badge sleeves swing like credentials were a kind of gravity.

In the hallway, she didn't look back toward the elevator bank.

She didn't need to.

Up here, nobody checked.

Nobody asked.

You could be anyone, as long as you looked like you belonged.

And now she knew what to do with that.

She pressed the access badge sleeve flat against her lapel and walked toward the next corridor as if she had been expected all along.

CHAPTER TWELVE

THE STRATEGY MEETING

A few days after Mara's corporate meeting on thirty-six, she sat in her hideout on seven with her notes and handouts spread out like a crime scene. The pages were glossy, heavy, expensive in a way that made you handle them carefully, even when they were nonsense. She had taken them from the last meeting on instinct, the same way she took receipts, counted drawers, counted steps, and wrote numbers down, even when the system said it already had them.

Last night, she read them three times.

The first pass was panic. The second was translation. The third was strategy.

She built herself a cheat sheet on a yellow legal pad. Names, titles, the order people spoke in, the phrases that made heads nod. Acronyms with guessed meanings. Some guesses wrong. She didn't care. The point wasn't to be right. The point was to sound like someone who had the right to be wrong in that room.

On her next day off from the café, when a fresh wave of black access badges drifted toward the nice elevators, Mara was ready. Half her week still belonged to the café. The rest of it, more and more, belonged to the Tower.

She wasn't behind the bar this time. The blazer fit a little better. The access badge sleeve was matte black, clean and anonymous, clipped where it caught the light. She carried an empty coffee mug as if she had just come from a coffee run that mattered.

She slipped in behind three executives as the doors slid shut. None of them looked at her. None of them needed to. The building had already decided who was allowed to exist in a small space together. The rest was manners.

The elevator rose without a sound. Mara watched their reflections in the mirrored panel. They spaced themselves without speaking. The tallest one took the center as if the elevator belonged to him. The others drifted to the edges with practiced deference, like a formation they learned before they learned their job titles.

The higher the floor, the less noise was required to assert control.

When the elevator opened on forty-eight, the last office floor before the executive suites, Mara counted heartbeats. One. Two. Three. She stepped out only after the last heel hit carpet and the doors began to close again.

Up here, sound was absorbed. The click of a heel. The dull scuff of rubber. Even the hiss of the HVAC died before it could echo. The air smelled like lemon polish and money, real money.

A receptionist waited at a glass-and-metal desk, posture perfect, hair shellacked to the curve of her skull. She wore an access badge that looked like jewelry and a smile trained to be small.

Mara walked up and did what she had practiced. Face bored. Body busy.

"Strategy session," Mara said, like it was an inconvenience.

The receptionist's eyes flicked to Mara's access badge sleeve. She didn't read the name. She scanned the silhouette.

"Conference room down the hall," she said, already turning back to her screen. "End of the hall."

Mara nodded once and kept moving.

The conference room was a terrarium of daylight and curved surfaces. A long wall of windows looked out over the city's east flank, catching cold sun and multiplying it against the glass. The walls that weren't windows were covered in acoustic paneling disguised as expensive felt. Everything was soft enough to swallow sound and sharp enough to cut you anyway.

Twelve seats. Five already full.

They were a different species up here. Same human bones, different rules.

A man in a checked sports coat typed without looking. He smiled at his screen like he was flirting with an email. A person in a black turtleneck bounced a knee under the table so hard the chair trembled. A woman in a suit so blue it left afterimages if you blinked, rearranged her papers into stacks, then destroyed the stacks with one irritated swipe and started over.

At the head sat Eleanor Sterling.

Mara recognized her from internal newsletters and the leadership posters in the lobby that nobody looked at unless they were new. In person, Eleanor looked less like a photo and more like a decision. Oxblood coat. Hair too precise to be accidental. Eyes that moved like they were reading the room the way Mara read the line at 7:22 a.m.

Eleanor was here to run the room.

A sideboard near the wall held a platter of croissants, an untouched bowl of fruit, and two stainless thermal coffee pots that looked like they came from a hotel where you weren't allowed to touch anything. Real coffee perfumed the air. Up here, caffeine came in porcelain mugs, not paper cups.

Mara's palms dampened around her empty mug. She set it down like it had always been there and chose a seat at the margin, half a chair from the end. Close enough to observe. Far enough to disappear.

A blank tent card sat in front of her with a marker.

Mara wrote MORGAN in neat block letters. Under it, smaller, OPS.

Her hand didn't shake. This was still handwriting. She could do handwriting.

Eleanor glanced down the table. Her gaze passed over Mara without snagging.

Mara exhaled.

Grace entered with a thin stack of printed pages and the expression of someone trained to look calm while holding a live wire. Her smile flickered when she saw Mara, relieved, like finding the correct puzzle piece.

"We're on time," Grace said briskly. "Thank you."

Eleanor tapped her phone once. The lights dimmed a fraction. The projector woke with a soft, expensive hum.

"Final pass," Eleanor said. "This is our Q2 scenario deck for leadership review. I expect questions. If you're here to agree, you can agree in an email."

A few people laughed, the way you laughed when you were supposed to.

Turtleneck stood and took the clicker as if it were a microphone.

"Slide one."

The deck moved.

Mara let the first slides blur past. Arrows. Flowcharts. Boxes that pretended to be systems. Vocabulary designed to make uncertainty sound like a choice. She wrote a few phrases on her pad and translated them without mercy.

Alignment: everyone says yes at the same time Mitigation: the lie we tell ourselves so we can sleep Risk table: the part where someone gets blamed

She didn't need to understand the whole deck. Her actual job was watching the room.

Eleanor's attention sharpened whenever someone hid behind a phrase. Sport Coat used jokes like sugar packets, sprinkling them over bitter slides to make the room swallow. Blue Suit looked up only when numbers changed, as if human voices were background noise and the only thing that mattered was what could be measured.

Then Eleanor stopped the clicker on a slide titled: MARGIN SCENARIOS: AGGRESSIVE vs DEFENSIVE.

"This is the number we'll be judged on," Eleanor said, tapping the screen with a stylus. "So let's stop lying to ourselves. What's the actual downside?"

Sport Coat smiled like he'd been waiting. "We modeled up to a two percent deviation. Beyond that, it's black swan territory."

Turtleneck nodded, eager. "We'd have to assume a total supply chain collapse for anything worse."

Eleanor didn't soften. "Supply chain collapsed last year. Are we pretending it won't happen again?"

A small laugh moved around the table, embarrassed and grateful that Eleanor made it a joke instead of a threat.

Turtleneck clicked forward. A risk table appeared. Jagged numbers. Ugly ones.

"What's the true floor?" Eleanor asked.

"Negative three, if everything goes against us," Turtleneck said. "But that assumes..."

"That assumes we live in a vacuum," Eleanor said. "We don't."

Sport Coat tried to rescue the mood. "There's political cover, though. Even if we tank, the optics..."

"Optics are my job," Eleanor cut in. "Numbers aren't. Stick to what we control. Or what we can report without Legal getting nervous."

Blue Suit spoke as if she'd been asked directly. "Negative five if you count cascading failures in contractor coverage. Most of that can be deferred into Q4. Nobody expects a hero. They expect a controlled collapse."

Nobody argued.

Mara wrote controlled collapse and underlined it twice. She didn't know why it made her angry. She just knew it did.

Eleanor nodded once. "Good. Put that in the summary as the real downside. Next. Facilities and services."

The next slide came up, and Mara felt her shoulders tighten: COST OPTIMIZATION: FACILITIES AND SERVICES.

Turtleneck clicked his tongue like he was about to tell a story. "We modeled the effect of the proposed night shift reduction," he said, tapping a green cell. "By shifting non-critical maintenance to day crew, we save just under one point five percent on margin with negligible impact on service delivery."

Negligible impact sat on the slide like a dare.

Eleanor's stylus hovered. "Pressure tested with Facilities?"

"They confirm feasibility," Turtleneck said. "As long as the day crew gets a small labor uptick. We build that into the run rate."

Sport Coat leaned in, suddenly serious. "Any risk of deferred maintenance stacking up? Like last year?"

Turtleneck waved a hand. "Model says no. Automation. Efficiencies."

Mara stared at the slide. She didn't see the building they were describing. She saw Janis's mop cart. Sammy's leak note. A jammed faucet. The HVAC vent full of muffin. The constant small failures held together by people who didn't get to sit in this room.

She waited for Eleanor to press.

Eleanor didn't. Eleanor was watching the room, not the cell.

The clicker advanced, and the story smoothed itself again.

Mara felt the urge to let it pass. It wasn't her job. It wasn't her slide.

Then Turtleneck said, "Morgan, you have the latest on building coverage, right?"

He looked straight at her as if her name had always existed.

Mara's heart did one hard kick.

She didn't panic. Panic made you loud. Mara had survived twenty years of loud.

She looked down at her handouts and found her own handwriting.

Night coverage already reduced. Access badge gaps. Work order backlog by week six.

She looked up.

"Yes," Mara said, and her voice came out even.

She heard herself speak and thought, Who's that?

"They're modeling off last year's baseline," Mara continued. "Night staffing is already down. If you cut again, it doesn't slope. It drops."

Turtleneck frowned. "Based on what?"

"Based on your own deck," Mara said, and tapped the paper. "Slide eight assumes full waste-handling cycles. That cycle already misses. When it misses, the work order line gets noisy. The system flags back up. Then Security starts asking why the access badge logs don't match headcount."

The room held still for a second, the way it did when someone said a thing out loud that everyone had been pretending wasn't real.

Sport Coat glanced at his laptop and made a small sound. "She's not wrong."

Blue Suit looked fully awake. "If that's true, the savings are inflated."

Turtleneck's jaw tightened. "That isn't what the summary said."

Mara shrugged once, small. "The summary is optimistic."

Eleanor leaned back and studied Mara.

"Can you support that?" Eleanor asked.

Mara kept her answer brief. "Facilities weekly staffing note. Work order line volume. Access badge gaps after midnight."

Eleanor turned to Turtleneck. "Rerun it. Fix the slide. Don't give Audit a reason to look at us."

Turtleneck's face went flat. He clicked and typed harder than necessary. A green cell became red. The projected savings halved itself.

No one apologized. No one thanked Mara. The meeting didn't miss a beat. The number changed, and the room accepted the new number as if it had always been the truth.

Mara wrote: They only believe what is projected.

Coffee mugs around the table began to run low.

Mara stood without thinking. Crossed to the sideboard. Wrapped her hand around the nearest thermal pot. It was heavier than the lobby ones, but the balance was the same.

Tilt. Pause. Half inch from the rim.

Muscle memory did the rest.

She filled Sport Coat's mug. Then Turtleneck's. Then Blue Suit's.

"Thanks, Morgan," someone said, casual, as if her name had always belonged in this room.

Mara froze with the pot mid-tilt.

Eleanor didn't slide her mug forward. She just watched.

Mara set the pot down slowly, exactly where it had been, and returned to her seat with her face composed and her pulse loud.

Eleanor's voice stayed light. "You don't have to do that."

Mara smiled, polite, the one she used when customers complained about foam. "Habit," she said.

Then, because panic made her stupid, she added, "I was doing a quick caffeine distribution check."

The room laughed.

Eleanor nodded once. "Good. Keep the stakeholders resourced."

Mara smiled like it was normal. Inside, something sank. She had just proved she belonged, and she had also proved what she didn't.

The deck continued. Properly caffeinated, the room pretended not to notice how natural it had felt to let her serve them.

When the agenda hit INCIDENT RECAP, Eleanor's attention sharpened.

"This is the part that can become public," she said. "So, we'll treat it like it matters. Julian."

A man appeared at the midpoint of the table as if he'd been there the whole time. Dark suit. Clean teeth. Eyes that never stopped scanning. Public Affairs moved like smoke.

"We have a viral event," Julian said, and the room straightened. "The White Tablecloth clip passed two million views. External accounts are tagging us."

He let that hang.

"The risk isn't the footage," Julian continued. "The risk is the narrative. We're being painted as vulnerable and easily breached. Someone called it a metaphor for invisible labor. That isn't a metaphor we want trending."

Sport Coat snorted. "Are we really doing this? A ghost crisis?"

A few people laughed nervously.

Julian didn't laugh. "If we get ahead of it, it becomes harmless office folklore. If we don't, it becomes a union talking point or a shareholder embarrassment. We don't let the outside world write our internal story."

Eleanor tilted her head. "So, we write it?"

Julian nodded. "We contain it. Reframe it as an internal security test. Push an employee engagement angle. Make it a controlled joke."

Turtleneck tried for charm. "Maybe we should hire the Phantom. At least she gets things done."

The room nervously laughed.

"She?" Eleanor said, surprised. The laughter stopped instantly.

Turtleneck blinked. "Rick thinks it's female."

Mara stared at the slide. UNAUTHORIZED PRESENCE. The words sat there, clean and simple, as if the problem were that a person existed in the building without permission, not that the building had become a place where existing required permission.

They spent ten minutes discussing how to make the story disappear.

When Eleanor finally closed her tablet, the meeting collapsed in on itself. Chairs scraped softly. Jackets shifted. People said good deck and solid numbers as if the deck were a person who needed praise.

Grace slid updated handouts down the table. Mara took one, tucked it into her blazer pocket with the same care she used for receipts. Then she took a second and tucked it behind the first.

No one noticed. Everyone was already late for something else.

Sport Coat tapped her shoulder as she passed. "Thanks for flagging the Facilities issue," he said, casual, like he was thanking her for holding a door. "Could have been embarrassing."

"It's always the small stuff," Mara said.

He chuckled and returned to his phone. "See you next round."

Mara nodded as if she belonged to the phrase.

In the hallway, the Tower's nervous system thrummed under polish. Somewhere, a copy of her face would end up in a directory. Somewhere, a rumor about her would be tweaked for maximum efficiency.

She didn't rush. Rushing was for people who could be questioned.

She took the elevator down with a trio of managers talking loudly about lunch reservations at places Mara could not afford. Nobody acknowledged her.

On the lobby level, she didn't go toward the café. She didn't look at the Phantom Watch board. She didn't check whether Marcy's drawing was still curling at the edges.

She walked like a person who had been paid to be on forty-eight and now had somewhere else to be.

***

At the gym, she slipped into the locker room and locked herself into a stall. She peeled off the blazer and blouse and folded them into a plastic bag. Her café uniform waited underneath, black polo and khakis like a punishment that fit.

She changed in silence. Her hands moved automatically, the ritual as old and numbing as pulling espresso.

When she was back in her own skin, she tucked the meeting handouts deeper into her bag, under the uniform she had just removed, and ran cold water over her wrists until her pulse steadied.

Then she went where she always went when she didn't want to be seen.

The service elevator answered the Morales access badge with a soft green blink. It carried her past safe floors and let her off where nobody important ever went on purpose.

Seven.

The under-construction seventh floor greeted her with its familiar chill. The temporary camera gone. Drywall stacks. Plastic sheeting. The faint chemical tang of fresh paint that never fully cured. Mara slipped through the gap she had made and into the nest she had carved out of insulation and tape.

She pulled the handouts out and spread them on the floor in front of her.

In the quiet, away from polished glass and polite laughter, the pages looked like confession. Risks. Cuts. Optics. Narratives.

Mara traced a line item with her finger and let herself breathe.

Day off, she thought.

Just a different shift.

She lay back, eyes on the unfinished ceiling, and listened to the building settle. Upstairs, they were already revising the story. Downstairs, Marcy was making coffee. In between, on seven, the Phantom studied what the Tower said about itself when it thought nobody was listening.

CHAPTER THIRTEEN

THE CORPORATE JET

O n her next day off, Mara went higher.

    She spent six minutes staring at herself in the gym bathroom mirror, testing whether the outfit would pass without a second look. The blazer and shirt came from the fitness center's lost-and-found, left behind by consultants who treated the gym as a ritual. The blazer was a size too big, the shirt mostly fitted, and the black pants could pass for any of a dozen business casual standards if no one looked too closely.

That was the point. She was starting to believe the Tower would let her.

She folded her café uniform, a faded black polo with a grease stain on the cuff, into her bag and zipped it tight. Even now, her hands wanted to smooth a bar towel, to touch the familiar edges of her apron, but this outfit demanded different movements. Straighten the cuffs. Flatten the shirt. Check the pocket for a notepad she didn't have.

She slung the bag over her shoulder and stepped back into the corridor, ready to see how far the Tower would let her go this time.

The elevator up was empty. Mara watched the numbers climb and ran her play in her head, clean and simple. Show up. Take the seat at the end. Don't talk unless spoken to. Blend.

The day's first meeting was a nonstarter. Budget. Metrics. A hundred slides of fake numbers. Mara logged her presence, answered one question about maintenance as a "contingent consultant," then faded into the room's noise. When it wrapped, she ducked into a side corridor, already mapping the path back down to seven and the quiet concrete where she actually slept.

Instead, she walked straight into a woman with a buzzcut and a clipboard.

"You're on this deck, right?" the woman said, scanning the roster. "Ops, Facilities, Transition Support?"

Mara hesitated for half a second. "Yes."

"Good." The woman made a neat check on the page. Her access badge read T. CARLSON, EXECUTIVE COORDINATOR. "We could use you on this trip. Black van, curb in five. Bring a laptop or pretend you forgot it."

Mara opened her mouth, then shut it. There was nothing to say that wouldn't sound like no, and no wasn't an option.

Carlson was already walking away, calling names Mara didn't recognize.

Mara followed the arrows to the lobby.

***

Outside, the curb ran like a staging line. A black van idled with its door open. Town cars waited behind it, drivers leaning on their hoods and trading rumors with small, economical gestures. People in coats that looked like uniforms without being uniforms hovered near the door, pretending they weren't watching the order of entry.

Carlson stood at the open side door, phone to her ear, clipboard in the other hand. "We are wheels up in ninety, so let's not screw around," she said to nobody Mara could see, then pointed with the clipboard. "Ops seat is yours."

Inside, the van smelled faintly of leather and cold air. Two women in near-identical trench coats had become precise silhouettes of bone and perfect teeth. A man in a suit sat with his eyes half closed, thumb flicking through his calendar. A younger guy in startup jeans and a Henley hunched over his phone. A woman with a platinum bob and an access badge full of access levels watched the others with polite boredom.

Mara slid into the back seat beside a duffel bag and kept her posture loose and unremarkable. The startup guy gave her a brief smile, then went back to his screen. Mara set her phone on her knee, screen black, as if answering a text.

The van pulled away from the curb.

Carlson leaned over the back of the driver's seat. "Quick intros. We're running point for the Westmont handoff. Ops in the back is covering facilities and transition. If you don't know each other yet, you're behind."

The platinum bob reached her hand back without turning. "Tess. Brand Strategy."

Her shake was perfect, firm enough to register.

The man in the suit nodded once. "Ty."

The two trench coat women spoke in turn. "Sharon. Planning." "Liv. Compliance."

The startup guy added, "Jordan. Data science," and winced at how eager it sounded.

Mara nodded. "Ops," she said, nothing more.

Nobody asked for a name. That was a relief.

The city smeared past the windows. Glass, brick, steel, then a run of chain link and loading docks as the van cut toward the airport's private entrance. The transition from downtown to perimeter security happened fast. A gate. A service road lined with company shuttles and rented SUVs. Then a terminal smaller than Mara's old apartment building.

Inside, the air was overcooled and filtered within an inch of its life. Giant screens looped weather maps and muted business news. Everything looked clean enough to be disposable.

Carlson moved them through security with muscle-memory efficiency. "Access badges visible. Anything metal into the bin. Pretend you've done this before."

The execs had. Coats came off before the checkpoint. Shoes chosen for speed, not fashion, even if they managed both. Laptops appeared in perfect choreography, no stickers, no dents. Even Jordan had a rhythm; he fumbled the tray, recovered, and threw the guard a shy grin.

Mara emptied her pockets except for her access badge sleeve. The guard barely glanced at it. Her bag went through. So did she. Nobody stopped her to ask why an ops consultant with a cheap blazer was boarding a corporate jet.

On the far side, Carlson handed out tiny bottles of water. "Boarding in twenty."

The lounge felt more like a holding pen than luxury. Rows of chairs. A wall of outlets. A fridge of generic seltzer. Packaged snacks arranged to look like generosity. Tess and Ty claimed a table and started sketching on a legal pad. Sharon and Liv found a corner and dropped their voices to discuss persona decks and message discipline. Jordan sat by the window and frowned at an article on his phone.

Mara drifted to a shelf lined with books nobody had touched in years. Management texts. Obsolete legal codes. The company's official history with its dust-faded cover. She pulled one at random and sat with it open in her lap.

From there, she could see the whole room without being seen. People moved in pairs. Every pause in conversation was only a setup for the next small negotiation. Even the way they drank water signaled something, nerves or control.

Carlson clapped her hands once. "Let's move. We are first out."

They formed a line without needing instructions. Ty in front. Tess on his left. Sharon and Liv behind them. Jordan, then Mara at the end, the borrowed blazer suddenly feeling twice as heavy.

They walked the jetway as a single organism, each on a phone or talking in low tones. Carlson peeled off at the last door and surrendered her clipboard to a ground staffer without breaking stride.

The plane itself felt unreal, smaller than Mara expected. Two rows of wide leather seats, half already occupied by people in the same quiet uniform of status. The air smelled of old leather and new money.

Mara took the last open window seat, buckled herself in, and arranged her body like she did this every week. She tried to pretend this wasn't her first time on an airplane.

As the engines spooled up, she shut her eyes and gripped the armrests. The pressure shifted as they roared down the runway and lifted off.

She told herself she belonged there at least until they landed.

When the plane leveled, the cabin settled into a soft storm of keyboard taps and notification chimes. Mara kept her gaze on the glass, not the clouds, just the steady slab of blue beyond them. She counted heartbeats and didn't like the total.

She sensed the woman before she saw her. A presence in the aisle, a rustle of fabric, then Eleanor Sterling slipped into the seat beside her, tablet in one hand, a small bottle of mineral water in the other. Suit charcoal. Scarf the color of milk. Hair pulled back in a loose knot that looked effortless and probably took ten minutes in a mirror.

Eleanor didn't look like anyone's plus-one. She looked like someone who could fire a CEO and still make the board thank her for it.

They sat in silence for a dozen heartbeats. The plane roared. The vents hissed.

"You were at the meeting a few days ago," Eleanor said eventually.

It sounded more like a statement.

Mara nodded, careful.

"I always wonder what it feels like from the edges," Eleanor went on, twisting off the cap of her water. "All those careful decks. The optimism we sell to ourselves."

Mara gave a small, crooked smile. "I'm usually invisible. That's the point."

Eleanor turned her head and studied her. "In my experience, the invisible ones are the only people who ever know what's actually happening."

Two rows ahead, Jordan had already drifted into a noisy sleep. Tess and Ty whispered a string of words that all sounded like parts of a presentation. Deck. Offset. Optics.

Eleanor reached into her jacket pocket and pulled out a small metal tin. She flipped it open and held it between them. "Mint?"

The mints were lined up like tiny white coins. Mara hesitated, then took one. It was sharper than she expected, a clean sting of peppermint that cut through recycled air.

"Press conferences are easier if your mouth isn't dry," Eleanor said. "Even for the people who never stand at the podium."

Mara frowned. "Press conferences?"

"Westmont has an optics problem," Eleanor said calmly. "A local incident. Minor in the grand scheme. Noisy in the wrong channels. We're going out to help them remember the approved version of events."

"PR containment," Mara said.

"You said that, not me." Eleanor's smile held no humor. "Officially, it's a listening tour and stakeholder engagement. Unofficially, we're there to make sure the story doesn't escape its enclosure."

Mara rolled the mint on her tongue until it settled in the hollow of her cheek. The sweetness felt like a marker she couldn't spit out later.

"You fly a lot," Eleanor said.

It wasn't a question.

"Only when they put me on the manifest by mistake," Mara said, and immediately wished she had chosen different words.

Eleanor's eyes shifted, small and quick, like she'd just put a pin in something. "Mistakes are often the best part of any trip." She looked past Mara, out at the sky. "I used to travel constantly. There was a stretch when I spent more nights in hotels than in my own bed. I can still picture the carpet in every generic business hotel between here and Shanghai."

"Do you still?" Mara asked.

"Not as much." Eleanor's voice dropped into something closer to honest. "Now I live in the Tower like everyone else. It feels like an airport hotel, though. Never quite day or night. Always in between."

Mara thought about the night floors, the silent elevator lobbies, the way the lights dimmed but never turned off. "The vents sound the same on every floor," Mara said. "Once you notice, you cannot unhear it."

Eleanor turned fully toward her. "You know the building better than most."

"Old habit," Mara said. "I started on the support side. It never really leaves you."

Eleanor's gaze didn't leave her face. "Support side where?"

There it was. Clean. Casual. A question dressed as conversation.

Mara felt her mouth go dry around the mint. "In the building," she said. "Early shifts. Back corridors. You notice things."

Eleanor nodded, as if that answered something and also didn't. "I always assumed the place ran on coffee and access badge scanners," she said. "You're telling me the vents are doing all the work?"

"And the alarms," Mara said. "You can tell time by them if you're stuck there long enough."

Eleanor watched her for a second too long. "Which floor are you based on?"

Mara's pulse climbed into her throat, quick and hot.

She kept her voice mild. "Wherever they put me."

Eleanor accepted that the way a person accepts a lie when they don't want to argue in public. "Flexible," she said.

The plane shuddered through a pocket of turbulence. Mara's fingers tightened around the armrest. Eleanor steadied her water bottle with two fingers and didn't flinch.

"You remind me of someone who used to work in the GSOC," Eleanor said once the cabin smoothed. "She got lost in the ducts during a system upgrade and claimed she could hear the whole building breathing. The engineers were furious."

Mara kept her eyes on the window.

Eleanor continued, voice even. "I thought she might be the only sane one in that underground dungeon."

Mara swallowed. "What happened to her?"

"Same thing that happens to anyone who notices too much," Eleanor said. "The story moved on without her."

It landed like a fact. The warning was inside it.

They fell into a quieter kind of talk after that. Weather. Airports. The way every city looked like broken circuitry from thirty thousand feet. Mara admitted she had never been west of the Rockies. Eleanor admitted she had never stayed in one place for more than a year before the Tower.

Eventually, the seatbelt sign chimed on. The engines changed pitch. Laptops snapped shut. Phones lit up with the first wave of emails from people who hadn't noticed their recipients were in the air.

"You see things most people ignore," Eleanor said suddenly. Her voice softened, but her eyes didn't. "That's rarer than it should be."

"It's just vents and carpet patterns," Mara said, trying to make it small.

Eleanor shook her head, amused. "If you say so."

Mara was left with the unsettling feeling of having been seen, then deliberately not exposed. The mercy felt temporary.

The wheels hit tarmac with a bounce that rattled her teeth. The spell of the flight broke at once. Ty was already on his phone. Tess and Sharon swapped into different shoes. Jordan shoved his laptop back into its sleeve like he could erase whatever he'd written.

Mara waited until the aisle cleared, then slid her bag down from the overhead without bumping a single suit.

They filed out in a neat order that mirrored some invisible chart. Carlson led. The others fell in behind her in rank order. The jet bridge emptied into a waiting room that looked like a high-end copy of the lounge back home, only smaller and more expensive. The air smelled like lemons and static.

A handler in a navy vest raised a clipboard. "Welcome to Westmont," he said, handing each of them a folder.

Inside Mara's, a single sentence was highlighted in yellow.

Ops: support as needed.

It felt like a punchline.

Outside, town cars and shuttles idled in a precise row. Carlson assigned rides with quick, surgical decisions. Tess and Ty in the first car. Sharon and Liv in the second. Jordan into a shared shuttle with two people Mara didn't know.

Mara was halfway to the last van, the one that had operations written all over it in subtle ways, when she heard a voice behind her.

"Excuse me."

She turned. Eleanor stood in the shade of the awning, phone in one hand, the mint tin in the other. She snapped it shut and slipped it into her pocket as their eyes met.

"I wanted to thank you," Eleanor said. "Not many people can travel this far and still keep track of the ground beneath their feet."

Mara searched for something neutral. "It's just vents and carpet patterns."

"Maybe," Eleanor said. The smile she gave then was the first real one Mara had seen from her. "Or maybe you just pay attention to what everyone else steps over."

There was a pause, long enough to feel like a choice.

"If you're ever in the building after hours," Eleanor added, "come up to the top floor. The view is different at night. The higher you go, the harder it is to hide."

Mara could only nod. Her throat had gone dry again, and her eyes had gone glossy.

Eleanor stepped away as if the moment hadn't happened at all. She slid into the back of a waiting car. The door shut with a soft, expensive click.

Mara walked to the van marked for ops staff. Two AV techs and a woman with a catering lanyard were already inside, staring ahead like they didn't want to see or be seen. Nobody spoke as the driver pulled away from the curb.

Out the window, a new city unspooled. Glass. Brick. Hotel towers. Chain link. Mara watched her reflection flicker across each surface, sometimes solid, sometimes fading out completely.

Nothing in her clothes or her access badge had changed since that morning. Inside, everything felt tilted. Eleanor hadn't confronted her. Eleanor hadn't accused her.

Eleanor had simply asked questions that would matter later.

The van merged onto the highway toward a regional headquarters Mara had only seen on slides. Mara closed her eyes and mapped the route in her head: every turn, every exit, every way back.

Even ghosts had to find their way home.

Eventually.

***

The Westmont building sat low and clean behind a gate, a glass cube surrounded by scrub grass and a parking lot full of rental cars. From the highway, it looked like any other regional office, an afterthought with an access badge reader. Up close, it was the Tower in miniature. Locked doors. Polished surfaces. People pretending they were calm.

Carlson ushered them through a side entrance where a local receptionist waited with a clipboard and a smile that never touched her eyes. "Welcome," she said, too bright. "Conference room is ready. Water and mints are set."

Mara followed the group down a corridor that smelled like new carpet and air freshener. The walls held framed photos of the building at different angles, sunrise and drone shots that made it look important. Someone had printed pride and put it in frames.

The conference room was larger than it needed to be. A long table. Too many chairs. A screen already glowing with a title slide: WESTMONT LISTENING SESSION STAKEHOLDER ALIGNMENT

Mara took a seat at the far end, close to the wall, close to the door. She set her folder on the table and opened it as if she belonged.

Ops: support as needed.

Support as needed was the company's way of saying you are here to do the heavy work and keep your mouth shut.

The local team filed in a minute later. A man with a damp collar and a too-tight smile. A woman with a legal pad clutched to her chest like it could protect her. Another man who looked like he hadn't slept. Two more people who tried to blend behind the first row. All of them wore the same expression Mara had seen in the Tower the morning after a sweep.

Something worse.

They had been told the story had already been decided.

Ty shook hands as if he were greeting donors. Tess flipped open her laptop with a practiced snap. Sharon and Liv sat together, shoulders aligned, compliance already in formation. Jordan hovered, then took a chair like he was bracing for impact.

Eleanor entered last.

The room shifted around her without anyone acknowledging it had shifted. The local manager stood a little straighter. The woman with the legal pad stopped fidgeting. Even Ty's posture changed, a small adjustment that said, noted.

Eleanor didn't sit right away. She walked to the head of the table and looked at the faces gathered there. Measuring.

"Good morning," she said. "We are here to be useful."

Carlson closed the door.

Mara sat very still, mint still sharp in her mouth, and realized the trip wasn't the risk.

The risk was that Eleanor now knew what kind of questions to ask.

And Eleanor had time.

CHAPTER FOURTEEN

PR CONTAINMENT

W estmont was supposed to stay there. A day of conference rooms, controlled sentences, and carefully arranged relief. Mara carried cables, coffee, and other people's urgency, and watched how a story got sealed shut before it could spread. By the time the jet brought them back, she could see the shape of what would come next. The same language. The same reassurance. The same quiet promise that everything was under control.

When the Tower acted like nothing had happened, she understood that meant the opposite.

Back in the Tower, the "Mandatory Safety & Security Forum" dropped into everyone's inbox at 7:12 a.m., a precisely worded slug of HR lingo and rainbow-colored clip art. The subject line used three exclamation points and the urgent emoji, as if safety were about to break into the building and rob them all at gunpoint.

Marcy read the email aloud while setting up the pastry case.

"It says here, 'We will review essential security best practices and address recent building-wide concerns in a positive, collaborative environment. All staff encouraged to attend.' Which means, 'We know about the Phantom and want you to shut the hell up about it.'"

Mara just nodded and kept slicing the cinnamon buns. Her shoulders still remembered the airplane seat from Westmont, but the dough didn't care.

"They're making us do table service for this one," Marcy went on. "In the atrium. It's not even a real conference. Just coffee and muffins and a bunch of scared execs pretending they're not sweating."

Mara shook her head. "No hats. It's a PR event, not a bake sale."

Marcy snapped on fresh gloves. "Hey, you think the Phantom will show up?"

"They'll probably search everyone at the door," Mara said.

Marcy grinned. "Good. Means they'll have to check the suits for a change."

***

The atrium had been scrubbed for the event. Glass polished until light doubled back on itself. Heaters stationed for the draft that never left. Branded bunting along the mezzanine railings read BRIGHTON HOLDINGS: SAFE TOGETHER, as if a slogan could keep a building stable.

New camera domes glinted above the crowd.

By 9:30 a.m., people drifted in wearing access badges like amulets. They clustered by department and watched the stage like it might start talking first. Facilities gathered near the garden wall in matching hoodies, posture both defiant and bored. Legal and HR filtered in late, tablets out, faces set in that meeting-expression that meant they were already writing an email in their heads.

Mara manned the coffee urns with her usual precision. Marcy bounced between stations, doling out muffins and opinions.

"You see the security setup?" Marcy whispered as she refilled a mug. "They brought in extra cameras. And look, Rick Holman is already pacing the back like a haunted Roomba."

Mara glanced up. Holman stood at the edge of the atrium with his badge on the outside of his blazer, hands folded behind his back, eyes sweeping the perimeter as if expecting a flash mob. He looked like a man trying to outlast a rumor by staring it down.

Janis rolled a mop bucket through the lobby, gave the rows of chairs a long, skeptical look, then vanished into a restroom with a grunt. Sammy sat near the Facilities cluster, thermos on his knee like a brace. He didn't speak much. He didn't need to. His presence said it all.

Marcy leaned in again. "Rumor says there's a surprise guest."

"Who?" Mara asked.

Marcy made a face. "Legal. Or maybe even Sterling."

Mara said nothing. The memory of Eleanor's statements pressed at her ribs. *The higher you go, the harder it is to hide.*

The lights dimmed slightly. A hush rolled across the room.

Mara wiped her hands, took her position behind the serving table, and watched the stage snap into focus.

The best seat in the house was always the one behind the curtain.

Julian Rhodes took the stage exactly on time. Director of Public Relations. Charcoal suit that reflected nothing. Tie sober enough to be approved by Legal and seasonal enough to be a lie.

He tapped the mic and waited for the echo to die. "Good morning," he said. "Thank you for joining us. I know it's not easy to carve time out of your day, but today is important. It's about keeping each other safe."

Marcy whispered, "I bet he practices in front of a mirror."

Julian smiled like he'd heard her and didn't care. The first slide lit up behind him: a stock photo of two hands clasped, both racially ambiguous, framed by BRIGHTON HOLDINGS: SECURITY IS TRUST.

Julian paced in a controlled arc. "Brighton is a place where people rely on each other. Whether you work on the fiftieth floor or down in the loading dock, our safety depends on vigilance and respect." He paused. "We're proud of our record. But even the best systems can be tested."

He advanced the slide. A cartoon burglar in a domino mask tiptoed past a vault.

A low, irritated laugh moved through the Facilities section.

Julian held up his hands in a gesture of transparency. "Many of you have heard stories. Some funny. Some alarming. About unauthorized activity in the building." He let the word unauthorized sit there like a scolding. "We take reports seriously. But it's important to understand that rumors can do more damage than reality."

Mara watched a woman in HR scribble the word FACTS in a notebook and underline it twice.

Julian clicked again. A simplified floor plan appeared, color-coded like a children's textbook. "Our Security Operations team, working with Facilities and IT, has audited access points and logs. We found no evidence of criminal intent or external breach. Most incidents were ordinary errors. Misplaced badges. After-hours cleaning. Delivery misroutes."

A man in a Facilities hoodie muttered, "Bullshit," and got a sharp elbow and laughter at the back of the room.

Julian smiled wider. "We know some of you still have concerns. We are not ignoring them. Starting next week, we are rolling out updated access protocols for contractors and vendors. Clearer rules. Better safety."

He paused with practiced sincerity. "And I want to address the elephant in the room. Or, as some of you have called it, the Phantom."

A ripple ran through the seats, half laughter, half challenge.

Julian air-quoted Phantom and chuckled. "Every building has its ghost stories. Ours is no different. But let's be clear. There is no threat. There is no shadow person in the walls."

The half-laugh that followed was nervous and angry at the same time.

Julian's voice softened. "If there were a real issue, you would be the first to know."

FACTS OVER FEAR appeared on the screen in the same font Mara had seen in the strategy deck and again over Eleanor's shoulder on the plane. Same lie, repackaged as comfort.

Janis, leaning against a column, raised one eyebrow and then went still again.

Julian closed with, "If you see something, say something. To Security. To HR. To your manager. Let's focus on what brings us together."

Polite applause. Tepid and obedient.

Julian smiled, satisfied, and stepped aside. "I'll hand it over to our Security Chief, Rick Holman, for specifics on updated protocols. Please give him a warm welcome."

Rick strode onstage as if the room were a perimeter.

Marcy, behind the coffee table, whispered, "Here comes the fun police."

Rick didn't waste time on stock photos.

His slide deck was navy blue and bullet points: ACCESS CONTROL UPDATE. AFTER-HOURS PROTOCOLS. INCIDENT REPORTING.

He advanced each line with the clicker, barely glancing at the screen.

"First," Rick said. "Building access is now access badge-only, twenty-four-seven. No tailgating. I don't care if you know the person behind you. If you let someone in, you're responsible for who comes through the door."

A few people shifted in their seats. A few looked away like children.

"Second," Rick said. "After-hours presence. If you're not scheduled, you don't belong in the Tower. No exceptions. Cleaning and Facilities will be double-logged. Security will conduct regular sweeps every two hours. Randomized."

Facilities didn't clap. They didn't move. Their stillness was its own response.

"Third," Rick said. "If you see something out of pattern, you report it to Security. No group chats. No Reddit. We have seen what happens when rumors get ahead of facts."

Somewhere on the mezzanine, a phone lit up with the White Tablecloth clip paused mid-drift. A suppressed laugh ran through a row and died.

Rick let it pass like he hadn't heard it. "As of this morning, there have been no confirmed breaches. The so-called Phantom is a social media artifact, not a verified threat." He said Phantom like it tasted bad. "Nevertheless, we are continuing our investigation. We'll identify the source of these incidents."

He didn't say we will protect you.

He said we will find them.

Mara felt the air tighten.

Rick clicked to his last slide: CAMERA COVERAGE EXPANSION. GARDEN. SERVICE CORRIDORS. STAIRWELLS.

"We are upgrading coverage," Rick said. "Some of you will notice new domes. Some of you will notice more access checks. Get used to it."

He ended with, "Security works when everyone does their part. If you aren't part of the solution, you're part of the problem."

Applause again, brief and obligatory.

Rick stepped back and crossed his arms at the side of the stage, eyes locked on the exits.

Marcy refilled cups and said, "He should sell tickets. I'd love to see him try to arrest a meme."

Mara poured coffee and watched the crowd. The talk was supposed to clamp down. Instead, people looked more awake. More charged. As if being told not to believe had made belief more tempting.

The next speaker, Legal by the look of her suit, launched into a monologue about privacy and oversharing. The room glazed over until the words disciplinary action appeared, then snapped back to attention.

The event dragged into an official Q and A.

A man from Facilities raised his hand and didn't wait to be called on.

"If there's no Phantom, and no threat," he said, voice even, "then why are we running sweeps, doubling logs, and installing new cameras overnight?"

The room went still in the way it did when someone asked a question that couldn't be softened.

Julian smiled first. He always did.

"That's a fair question," he said, nodding once, as if the word fair settled it. "And I want to be very clear. This isn't a response to fear. It's a continuation of best practices."

Rick didn't look at the man. He looked at the exits.

"Security isn't just about reacting to confirmed threats," Rick said. "It's about posture. Visibility. Accountability. When systems are stressed, we reinforce them."

"So it's preventative?" the Facilities man asked.

"It's responsible," Julian said smoothly. "And temporary."

A few people shifted in their seats. Someone in Legal wrote something down and crossed it out.

Rick added, "If there were a real danger, you wouldn't be hearing about it like this."

That landed wrong.

The Facilities man lowered his hand. He didn't look convinced, but he didn't push. That, too, was part of the system.

Around the room, people nodded the way they did when they understood the answer wasn't meant for them.

Mara poured coffee and watched the room absorb it.

They hadn't explained the cameras.

They hadn't explained the sweeps.

They'd explained why questions were the problem.

An over-caffeinated HR manager read questions from a printed stack, edges pre-censored. "How will updated access badge rules affect shared workspaces?" "Will there be more security in the parking garage at night?" "How do we report unusual behavior?"

Julian and Rick traded answers like a relay. Nothing to worry about. Safety is our priority. Report through the proper channels.

The Phantom hovered over every sentence like static.

Someone on the mezzanine tested the air with two loud syllables.

"Phan-tom."

A laugh popped and died. Another voice echoed it, half-joking, half-challenging.

"Phan-tom."

The word bounced off glass and came back bigger.

A third voice joined, then a fourth.

It was a question the room asked the room.

Then the rhythm caught.

"Phan-tom. Phan-tom…"

More people joined in, some grinning, some pretending they weren't. The sound rolled across the mezzanine and filled the atrium in waves. Relief, not rage. A room full of employees choosing a myth over a memo.

Julian's smile tightened, the corners held in place by training. Rick's jaw did the thing it did when he was deciding whether to clamp down or let it burn out.

In the front row, a few executives stood and slipped toward the exits, eyes forward, refusing to look like they'd been pushed.

Marcy caught Mara's eye and grinned like she'd found the pressure point.

Mara didn't move. She just listened, the chant rising and falling, and felt the building learn a new sound.

The HR manager tried to regain control. "Let's be respectful of everyone's time."

The chant didn't stop. It softened, then surged again, like waves finding the same shore.

"Phan-tom. Phan-tom…"

Rick stepped back toward the mic, shoulders set.

A radio chirped at his belt. Another chirped near the security ring.

"…GSOC wants faces from mezzanine. Start with the loud ones…"

Rick didn't say anything into the mic. He didn't have to. The order moved faster than speech.

Julian leaned toward the HR manager and said something through a tight smile. The HR manager nodded too fast.

The official Q and A collapsed. People stood and flowed toward the exits, still smiling, still repeating the word under their breath like it was a private joke.

The Tower had tried to seal the story.

The employees had opened it wider.

***

By noon, the café had become a rumor depot.

The Phantom Watch board was overflowing. New notes. New drawings. New offerings.

PHANTOM: 1, PR: 0 was underlined twice, the zero darkened until the paper puckered.

Someone left a black coffee and a bagel on the ledge labeled: OFFERING TO THE PHANTOM, DO NOT REMOVE.

Marcy stood in front of it with a marker like she was curating an exhibit. "They tried to kill it and made it bigger," she said, pleased. "It's science."

Mara wiped down the counter and watched the lobby drift back toward routine. People wore the chant like a grin. Even the ones who hated it couldn't stop referencing it.

Janis rolled her cart through and paused long enough to smirk at the board. "Good day for a haunting," she said softly.

"Maybe it's safer after they change the rules," Mara said.

Janis snorted. "Nothing's safer. It just looks that way on paper."

Sammy wandered in, grabbed coffee, and joined the cluster at the board. He didn't speak. He just watched, eyes narrowed the way they got when he was reading a system.

A security guard appeared near the corkboard and stayed too long, pretending to check his phone.

Then Maddy showed up.

Just Maddy, neat and awake, with a clipboard and a pen that never seemed to run out of ink. She stood at the edge of the café, as if it were her job to turn conversations into allegations and records.

She looked at the offerings, the drawings, the notes.

Then she looked at Marcy.

"Who started the chant?" Maddy asked.

Marcy blinked. "Oh my! Are we arresting syllables now?"

Maddy didn't smile. "Names. I want names."

Marcy shrugged with exaggerated innocence. "It was the building, babe. Acoustics."

Maddy wrote something anyway.

Mara watched Maddy's pen move and felt the room cool a degree. Maddy didn't threaten. She documented. Documents turned into records. Records got people TERMINATED.

Maddy's eyes flicked to Mara, then away, like Mara was a file she already had open.

"Behavioral escalation," Maddy said to nobody, voice flat.

Marcy leaned toward Mara and whispered, "She really does print feelings."

Mara didn't answer. She watched Maddy's clipboard.

Maddy tore off a small sticker from a sheet and slapped it onto the corner of the Phantom Watch board as if it were evidence tagged for storage: UNAUTHORIZED MATERIAL. DO NOT REMOVE UNTIL LOGGED.

Marcy squinted at the sticker. "If it's unauthorized, why not just take it down?"

Maddy didn't look up from her clipboard. "Because it gets collected later for processing. If you pull it now, you contaminate it."

Marcy frowned. "Contaminate. It's sticky notes."

"It's evidence," Maddy snapped. "And it's going in a file."

Mara watched Maddy's pen move. The Phantom had become the record.

CHAPTER FIFTEEN

THE TRAP

A t 6:04 a.m., Mara's phone vibrated with the urgent flag. The subject line ran three screens before it wrapped: UPDATED ACCESS CONTROL: AFTER HOURS POLICY: MANDATORY COMPLIANCE. The sender was a no-reply, the body all legalese and aggressive font. She read it three times, each pass revealing a new clause designed to trap somebody.

The gist was simple. Nobody in the Tower without an access badge. No propping doors. No courtesy holds for the next person down the hallway. All entrances would cycle into lockdown after 7:00 p.m. No exceptions. During business hours, it meant spot checks and new readers in the usual choke points. After 7:00 p.m., the building would lock hard.

She imagined the words as a thin blue line slicing the building floor by floor until you were either in or out, and nothing in between.

Marcy leaned over the back counter, chewing her straw. "You see this? They want us to badge into the bathrooms now." She squinted at her phone. "Okay, not all bathrooms. Just 'certain locations during non-business hours.' But still." She read from her phone with a dramatic lilt. "Due to recent events, all spaces will be access-controlled for your safety. Compliance will be monitored. If I die in a locked stall, it's on you to avenge me."

"Settle for a memorial on the espresso machine," Mara said, face blank.

"Only if you put flowers next to it."

Outside, the morning was half snow and half rain, the kind of light that made everyone inside the lobby look raw and unfinished. Mara started the shift the way she always did. Calibrate the grinder. Purge the line. Fill the pastry case. Her hands moved on muscle memory.

But today the rhythm snagged. Doors that used to swing and settle now thunked shut on timers. Access badge readers chirped louder, brighter, as if volume could replace reliability. Security officers hovered near the main doors watching for tailgaters, and Facilities staff cut through the lobby with tablets, scanning for the smallest sign of noncompliance.

By 7:10 a.m., the lobby's population had doubled. Wet jackets slumped in armchairs. Managers took calls at the communal table. The new rules were in effect.

At 7:17 a.m., a regular from Legal shook her head at the fresh signage. "It's like a prison, but with better coffee. Pretty soon, they'll want a DNA sample to use the microwave."

Mara offered a flat smile and glanced toward the entry line.

Just inside the threshold stood Sammy in a Facilities windbreaker, shivering despite the weight of his gear bag. He hovered with his eyes darting between the access badge station and the Security officer posted beside it, as if deciding whether coffee was worth the hassle.

Marcy waved him over. "We're doing repairs, or is this a social call?"

Sammy shrugged off his bag and slid onto a stool at the far end, palms pressed to the counter for warmth. "They sent an alert about a breaker.

Whole corridor near the mailroom is dead. But I have to badge through three checkpoints just to fix it."

"That's job security, right?" Marcy said, grinning.

Sammy's mouth twitched. "It's not security. It's a death wish. The mag locks are pulling double current. I can smell the relays from the elevator lobby."

"Smells like what?" Mara asked.

Sammy thought. "Burnt popcorn. Or ozone."

Marcy wrinkled her nose. "Gross. So how soon before we're all locked in for good?"

Sammy nodded toward the stairwell door. It thunked shut behind a passerby like it had been trained. "If they keep adding readers, maybe a week."

Mara watched the entrance. Rick Holman himself stood near the main reader, jaw set, eyes sweeping faces like he was counting them against a list he didn't have yet. Two officers tested the access badge station, pulled the door closed, and timed the lock. Less than two seconds. One nodded. The other typed into a tablet.

Mara handed off a cup, then drifted back toward Sammy. "How bad is it?"

He lowered his voice. "Everything's on one circuit because that's how the Tower was built. They're adding systems like we have infinite bandwidth. Last time they did this, the server room tripped at three a.m. and fried an access panel. Nobody got in or out for six hours."

"Was that the blackout week?" Marcy asked. "People were using the fire stairs to get between meetings. Total chaos."

Sammy grunted. "They never fixed the root problem. Now it's worse. I spent two hours yesterday flipping breakers so the GSOC could install new cameras, and nobody bothered to tell IT."

Marcy split a muffin and offered him the bigger half. "Eat something before you collapse. That's an order."

He took it, chewed, eyes still on the doors.

Behind him, the lobby performed its morning pageant. Badge. Scan. Proceed. Every third person struggled with the protocol. Access badges upside down. Credentials rejected. Confusion doubling back toward the garden entrance. Every face looked like it was waiting to be flagged.

Marcy glanced at the mess, then at Mara. "You think it'll ever go back to normal?"

Mara shook her head. "This is normal now. The Tower upgrades itself by subtraction."

Sammy leaned forward. "You ever hear the story about the old air handler on thirty-six?"

Marcy's eyes lit. "Please tell me it involves rats."

"No rats," Sammy said. "Just a service tech who tried to bypass a lock to fix a damper. System locked down, so she spent three hours in a shaft, ten degrees above freezing, with nothing but her phone and a water bottle. When they finally let her out, HR said she violated after-hours access policy. They made her write an incident report."

Marcy leaned in. "Did she write it as a ghost?"

"She quit," Sammy said. "But her name is on every warning in the service log now."

Mara watched Rick at the entrance again. When his gaze caught hers, he held it for a second too long, then moved on.

Marcy noticed. "He looks constipated."

"Probably is," Sammy said. "Old man eats more donuts than anyone I know."

Sammy pocketed the last bite, zipped his jacket, and hefted the gear bag onto one shoulder. "Supposed to meet Janis for the ladder, but she's not answering her phone."

"She hates the new rules," Marcy said. "Last night she called it a trap for the desperate."

"She's not wrong." Sammy started to move, then looked back once, the way he did when he wanted to say something without saying it. "If you see the lights flicker, get out. Might be the only warning you get."

Marcy snickered. "They're going to break this place before they catch anything."

Mara poured herself a black coffee. No sugar. She sipped and watched the doors thunk and seal and reset. Each new rule tightened the loop. Each new device created a new failure point.

The Tower was growing a new nervous system, and it already felt close to panic.

By early afternoon, the rush had thinned to a steady trickle. Mara scrubbed the counters, reset the case, and watched the lobby settle into its weekday posture.

***

Marcy left at 2:03 p.m., mouthing a drawn-out later and flashing a two-handed finger salute as she left. Mara stayed behind to finish the last steps. She wiped the final rings from the counter and lowered the gate halfway, a marker that the café was closed but not asleep.

The routine used to feel automatic. Now it felt like rehearsal.

Most nights, by the time evening settled in, Mara waited for the lobby lull. She watched for the east perimeter round. Then she slipped out of the side corridor and took the back stairs to the mezzanine. The second-floor janitorial closet cut to an old stairwell that was never locked and never checked. Two flights and a fire door, and she was on seven before the system knew she was gone.

Tonight, the air felt different the second she stepped into the service hallway. Colder. Sharper. A whiff of chlorine masking something more chemical. She kept her pace measured and hugged the tile edge, careful not to trigger the motion sensor that flickered the emergency lights overhead.

At the mezzanine access, the first break in the pattern hit her like a jolt.

The stairwell door that had been propped for years with a folded napkin or a strip of blue tape was now bare, shut, and newly dressed with a fresh access reader. Its tiny status LED pulsed green, patient and smug.

Mara lifted the Morales badge.

Yellow blink. Red.

She waited, counted to thirty, and tried again.

Yellow. Red.

A new plate had been bolted over the latch gap, too. No more carding the lock with thin metal. No more forgiving hinge. The door had been taught not to give.

Mara ducked into a side alcove, the supply closet where Janis once hid to dodge GSOC audits, and took stock.

The elevator was an option, but she never used it at night. Too exposed. Too many cameras. The exterior stairs were worse. Open sky meant a different alarm.

She checked her phone.

No signal in this pocket of the building.

Mara doubled back and tried the next stairwell. Unmarked. The door sat cracked open, as if someone had forgotten it.

She listened for footsteps, then pushed through.

Inside, the stairwell was silent and unlit except for exit signs at each landing. The acoustics were live. Every step echoed up and down the full stack of floors.

Halfway up the first flight, the building twitched.

The lights blinked once. The handrail vibrated with a quick ripple of current. Somewhere below, a mag lock thudded open and shut like a jaw.

Mara froze.

Then she moved, faster now, because she could feel the system straining in places she couldn't see.

At the fourth landing, she slowed and listened.

Voices. Two floors above, maybe less.

She pressed herself to the wall and waited. The voices carried.

"...said to sweep every level, even if nothing flagged. That's what Holman wants."

The reply was bored. "You think the Phantom's worth overtime? I'd rather catch a real break-in."

Security. Mara could tell by cadence alone. More swagger. Less patience.

She counted to fifty and let them finish their pass before moving.

At seven, she cracked the landing door and scanned the corridor.

A permanent camera at the far end, brand new, lens gleaming in the half light. Another reader beside the service door that used to be loose and indifferent. The old path past the janitor's cart and through the service access had become a funnel.

A kill box.

Mara closed the door and retreated back into the stairs to think.

The Tower had mapped her moves. Every shortcut had become a trap. Every corridor had become a funnel. The safe routes were turning into dead ends, one access badge reader at a time.

She went down to five and cut through a utility room that was hot, loud, and unmonitored. Pipes. Ducts. Wet concrete. She crawled under a low run, skirted a slick patch near a drain, and found the cross connection to the fire escape.

That door, at least, was still loose on its hinges.

She slipped through and reentered the seventh-floor construction zone from the back side.

Her nest waited where she left it, tucked behind drywall stacks and plastic sheeting.

She crawled inside, pulled her plastic blanket over her knees, and listened.

The Tower echoed around her. The metallic groan of elevator cables. The pulse of HVAC. Footfalls of night Security on the hunt.

She replayed every movement from the café to this hiding place. Every step had been riskier than the last. The old route was gone. The Tower had closed the grid behind her.

She was off the map now.

She would have to find a new way through.

She lay back and watched the red pinprick of an exit sign bleed through a slit in the wall.

Then, somewhere deeper in the building, the lights flickered.

Once.

Twice.

A stutter that felt like a warning traveling through the bones of the Tower.

Mara sat up, already moving, already listening.

From the corridor outside came a radio chirp, louder than usual, closer than it should have been.

"...Sweep team, tighten. He wants seven covered. Repeat, seven covered..."

Mara's throat went dry.

Rick wasn't guessing anymore.

The trap had a floor number now.

She pulled her knees in, pressed her ear to the drywall, and mapped the next move in the dark while footsteps began to climb.

CHAPTER SIXTEEN

IGNITION

The Tower was closing its seams. Night routes that used to forgive her now clicked shut behind her. If she wanted to stay inside, she couldn't keep moving like a ghost. Being the Phantom was getting harder. Being Morgan was getting easier. That didn't mean the Phantom was gone. It meant she could wait.

The camera on seven stayed. Janis made sure it didn't matter. A cart appeared when Mara needed to move, parked with the same careless precision as before, blocking the lens just long enough to turn a corridor into a blind spot. Janis never looked at her. She didn't need to. The system logged movement. It never logged intention.

On her next day off from the café, Mara made it down to the gym to prepare for a meeting upstairs. She stood in the gym bathroom and stared at herself in the mirror for six minutes, long enough to feel the disguise settle into her posture. Borrowed blazer. Borrowed shirt. Black pants that passed as business casual if nobody looked too closely. Her café uniform sat folded in her bag like a backup identity she could put on and disappear into. One let her belong. The other let her disappear.

She washed her hands twice, dried them, and checked the access badge in its sleeve. The face on it didn't belong to her. The plastic did. The Tower stopped asking questions as long as the right rectangles flashed green.

When she stepped back into the corridor, the air tasted wrong. Sharp. Electrical. This came from vents pushing air that had scraped along hot metal and dust. She had smelled it before, faint, in the service levels. That smell never stayed small.

She headed for the elevators without rushing. People who rushed got remembered.

The elevator carried her up in silence. She watched the numbers climb and kept her expression neutral, as if she had a calendar full of other people's problems.

She did.

She didn't look down at the floors passing beneath them. She knew what was down there. The café. The line. Marcy's voice cutting through the morning. The Tower would keep chewing, whether anyone noticed or not.

The day's first meeting blurred the way they always did. Budget. Metrics. A deck full of optimism that kept moving even when nobody believed it. Mara sat at the end of the table, nodded at the right moments, and said nothing unless someone pointed at her.

***

After the first meeting, she slipped out with the others and walked the corridor as if she belonged there. She kept her face calm and her gait steady. In every patch of glass, she caught her reflection, and for a second, she saw the split. Barista hands. Executive disguise. Same body. Two lives stacked on top of each other.

She rode down to the lobby and cut along the café's edge. She didn't step behind the counter. She didn't clock in. She just watched.

The café looked busy in the familiar way. A line. A drip machine. Wet jackets shaking water onto marble as if it were someone else's problem. She caught Marcy moving fast behind the bar, sleeves rolled, mouth running. Marcy looked tired. Everyone looked tired.

No one recognized Mara in the blazer. The Tower didn't read people. It read uniforms, lanyard colors, and access badges.

Mara tasted the air again. The sharp bite hadn't gone away. The building was complaining, and when the building complained, locks followed.

At 10:12 a.m., it was time for her next meeting. Mara checked her reflection in the glass, adjusted the access badge, and walked to the elevator without hurrying.

The ride to eleven was slow and jerky, pausing twice between floors for no reason. When the doors opened, she caught a whiff of lemon cleaner overlaying something harsher. Burnt plastic, faint but present, like a warning someone tried to bury under polish.

Two paralegals stood at the far end of the corridor with their faces parked in their phones. The lights above the elevator flickered, then stabilized.

Mara walked down the hall, one hand brushing against the wall, feeling for vibrations through the paint and drywall. An access badge reader blinked yellow instead of green. A red printout beside it said OUT OF SERVICE, USE MAIN ENTRANCE. Someone had scribbled below it: Or just pass through the walls, like the Phantom.

Near a reception desk, an admin greeted her without looking up. "Hey, you made it. Wasn't sure the elevators would."

"They work if you talk nicely to them," Mara said.

The admin half-smiled and nodded toward a conference room. "The meeting's down the hall, on the right."

Mara nodded, walked on, and stepped into a room full of laptops and bottled water. People spoke in careful phrases and pretended the slides meant something. Mara took a seat where nobody would remember her and kept her eyes on the lights instead of the deck.

A strobe hit once overhead. Barely a second. Enough to make the eye register a glitch. Nobody commented. They didn't want problems to be real until a manager named them.

When the meeting broke, Mara slipped out with the group, then peeled away into a side corridor to avoid the crowd. Narrower. Storage closets. HVAC returns. Halfway down, a door alarm chirped, then died. The silence was loud, like the system tried to speak and decided it wasn't worth the effort.

She stopped at the corner and listened. Nothing. Only the rattle of an air vent cycling through, then failing with a metallic thunk.

At the elevator bay, two Facilities guys in matching polos leaned over a wall panel and poked at a loose switch.

"Dead again?" Mara asked.

The older one grunted. "Building's a mess today. Power faults up and down."

"Anything dangerous?"

He shrugged. "Not unless you like surprises. Half the readers are on the fritz. Probably a short somewhere."

The younger one said, "They always do this. Patch one thing, break three. Place is held together with tape."

Mara nodded. The elevator arrived late. The lights inside looked dimmer than before.

She rode down and tried to breathe normally. She caught the smell again. Acrid. Faint. Like overheated wiring. Not enough to send people running. Enough to make the air taste like worry.

Back on the lobby level, she walked past the café instead of into it. Marcy glanced up from the register and looked past her. Marcy didn't see her in this outfit. That was the point.

Mara stopped near the edge of the lobby and watched the access badge readers blink. Green. Yellow. Green again. The lights pulsed, then steadied. Somewhere above, a fan rattled to life and died.

She didn't like the pattern.

***

The mechanical room on sub-two was supposed to run cool. It didn't. Heat shimmered above the relays, bending the air. A honeycomb panel mapped every circuit in the Tower. Green meant safe. Amber meant strain. Red meant failed.

Amber bled into red.

At 12:07 p.m., the access badge entry circuit on the east elevators spiked. The mag-locks didn't buzz. They screamed. The whine rose until a status diode faded from green to dead. Ten seconds later, a backup relay tried to take the load and tripped out with a pop loud enough to echo into the hallway. The system reset, limped, and reset again.

In the GSOC, Maddy noticed first.

"Fault in the east stack," she said, eyes on the panel. "Access badges not responding. Timestamp it. Get Maintenance down there."

"Push the reset," a voice answered from the next console. "They do this on warm days."

Maddy didn't look up. "Log that instruction."

The operator hesitated, then complied.

Maddy watched the reset attempt fail in slow increments. Amber bled into red. A status window blinked, froze, then populated with warnings that scrolled too fast to read. She screen-captured it anyway and opened a new incident file.

"And start a list," Maddy said, calm as paperwork. "Who ignored protocol this morning. Who held doors. Who moved without a schedule. When this becomes a report, it will need names."

Below, in a service corridor, Sammy saw a panel go dark. He swore under his breath and hit the override, the last resort. Lights came up. A burnt-sugar smell followed. Static crackled near the relay, a thin arc snapping from chassis to casing.

"No," he said, once. Then he keyed his radio. "Live short. Recommend isolating power now."

In the GSOC, Maddy marked the transmission and flagged it as an escalation.

The line crackled and went dead.

The alarm sounded wrong.

The normal alarm was steady and piercing, a tone that drilled through every wall. This one came in chopped bursts, like corrupted audio. Three short beeps. A pause. Nothing. The speakers tried again and produced a thin warble before failing back to silence.

Maddy frowned at the inconsistency. She pulled the alarm log and watched timestamps stack out of order.

"Document that," she said. "Alarm behavior deviates from standard."

Back in the lobby, two analysts rushed past Mara, talking too loudly.

"Smells like burnt electronics on nine," one said. "It's getting worse."

Mara didn't hesitate. If nine was filling with smoke, people would wait for an email that might never come. If the alarm panel was failing, doors might start choosing for them.

She got into the elevator and pressed nine. The elevator rattled as it climbed. When it stopped, the doors shuddered and opened halfway, as if the motor had lost interest.

Mara slipped through the gap and stepped into the corridor just as two office workers cracked their doors open.

"Is that a drill?" one asked.

"We're not due for a test until next quarter. Besides, drills don't come with smoke," the other said.

Mara leaned into the hall and listened. The ceiling speakers sputtered. "Attention, please," a voice tried, then dissolved into static.

She checked her phone. No alert. No instructions.

The lights stuttered again and switched to red emergency strips.

"Should we evacuate?" someone asked.

"Wait," Mara said. She listened. The alarm triggered again somewhere above, faint and unsynced.

A Security officer rounded the corner, face flushed. "Nobody panic. Maintenance says it's a glitch."

Mara smelled insulation now. Hot. Real.

"If it's a short, the fire panel could be dead," she said quietly.

The guard nodded. "I know."

Above them, smoke curled from a vent.

Mara made her choice.

She went up via the staircase.

Mara hit the first door with the flat of her hand.

"Fire," she said.

A man cracked the door, irritation already loaded. "We haven't gotten any instructions yet."

"Fire," Mara repeated. "Stairs. Down."

He hesitated, phone half-raised, waiting for something official.

"There won't be an email," Mara said. "Go."

That did it. The door opened wider. Voices rose behind him.

On the next floor, she didn't waste time explaining.

"Fire. Stairs. Down. Now."

A woman tried to argue. "My laptop—"

"Leave it," Mara said. "If you stop moving, you're not going to make it."

The woman stared at her, then turned back into the room and started waving others out.

On the next landing, the alarm stuttered and died again. The lights pulsed like they couldn't decide what to be. Mara didn't slow. She moved faster.

Some doors opened on the first knock. Some took three. Some people froze with their phones out, staring at blank screens.

Mara pointed at the stairwell. "Down."

A man asked, "Where do we go?"

"Outside," Mara said. "Keep going until the air changes."

She didn't wait to see if they listened. She just kept climbing.

At every floor, she knocked and yelled Fire. She sent people down the stairs, not waiting, not asking.

Move. Down. Out.

She climbed until her legs burned and the Tower groaned around her. She didn't stop.

Until the building emptied.

Or until she did.

By the time she hit fourteen, the alarms were failing more than they were sounding.

The stairwell door above her was hot to the touch.

Mara pulled her hand back fast and stared at the metal like it had spoken.

Behind her, the stairwell filled with footsteps coming down.

She looked up. Smoke pushed under the door seam in a thin gray line.

The Tower had turned into a chimney.

And she was still inside it.

CHAPTER SEVENTEEN

THE PHANTOM LEADS

T he alarms on fourteen had already given up, droning a half-hearted warble between longer stretches of silence. Mara took the last flight in a sprint, lungs burning, every landing a new taste of chemical haze. The smoke here was lazier, denser, rolling in through seams in the cinderblock like the Tower was exhaling from its wounds.

She didn't keep sprinting. Sprinting was for the first thirty seconds. After that, you picked a pace you could hold and you held it.

Her eyes watered, but she didn't stop.

Mara heard the chaos before she saw it: voices overlapping, a woman's sharp "Don't touch it!" followed by the slam of something metal. Three people clustered at the landing: two men in mismatched blazers, one already stripped to his undershirt and tie, and a younger woman with an access badge hanging from a lanyard and her phone gripped white-knuckled in one hand.

The source of their panic was obvious. The exit door was sealed, and the access badge reader glowed the wrong color: amber instead of green. The handle was blackened at the tip. The bravest of the men had tried it anyway, and now cradled his palm, lips pressed tight to keep from howling.

Mara saw all this in the instant before they saw her. When they did, the trio looked at her the way lost hikers look at a rescue chopper: desperate, hopeful, suspicious of miracles.

"Don't touch the handle," Mara said, voice flat but carrying. "It's live."

"We know," said the woman, coughing. "It burned him. Can we break it down?"

"Doubt it," Mara said, already moving past to inspect the door. She squatted, checked the hinge, the sweep, the seam where the frame met concrete. The heat radiated through her knuckles. It was hotter on the other side, which meant fire in the wall, or an electrical chase cooking itself to death. Or both.

"How did you get up here?" asked the younger man. His tie was cinched tight, his breathing ragged, every word coming through his nose.

"Stairs from the lobby. South core." Mara eyed the corridor behind them, smoke now thick enough to blur the exit sign at the far end. "You need to move. Now."

"Security said to shelter," said the first man, still holding his hand. "We waited ten minutes. Then the lights went out, and—"

"Security's wrong," Mara interrupted. Her throat burned from smoke and shouting, raw enough that the word came out harsher than she meant. "You wait, you cook. The other side is pulling air. This whole stack's gonna flood in smoke in five."

She pointed past them toward a door labeled MAINTENANCE ONLY. "Through there. It loops to the secondary service corridor."

The woman hesitated. "Are you sure?"

"I live here," Mara said. It wasn't a lie. "Go."

They went. Mara took the rear, pulled the other man's tie loose, and wrapped it around the burned hand as a makeshift bandage. Then she guided him forward. They moved as a single unit through the copy room, a tight rectangle of humming printers and half-spilled memos. The lights flickered but stayed on. A painting of a ship in a storm hung crooked on one wall, its frame tilted as if it might fall.

The group hesitated at the far door, which read AUTHORIZED ONLY. The woman eyed Mara.

Mara nodded once. "It's fine. Just go."

They plunged into the service corridor, and immediately the world changed. The noise dropped by half, the air a little cooler, the lights a sterile white. The hall was lined with janitor's closets and unmarked steel doors, each one with a different reader, none of them in use.

At the first junction, the group slowed again. "Which way?" the woman asked.

"Left," Mara said, "then down two." She kept her words clipped, matching the rhythm of their panic. "There's another stairwell that's not on the map. Maintenance only. The alarms don't reach that far."

They hustled down the corridor, their footsteps loud on bare concrete. Mara risked a glance back. The smoke in the office suite was now advancing through the open copy room, hungry for oxygen, each pulse a little thicker than the last.

She sped up, nearly pushing the group ahead of her. The woman fumbled her phone, tried to dial out, but the call failed; no bars, or maybe just the world deciding it was too late for outside help.

At the end of the hall, the door to the maintenance stairwell was propped open with a metal wedge. Someone, maybe Janis or Sammy, had been through here already, thinking ahead. Mara pulled the wedge, motioned the others inside, then reseated it on the inner edge to keep the latch open.

They started down the stairs, the burned man moving slowly, his other hand gripping the rail.

At the next landing, he stopped and looked at Mara with an exhausted, pleading expression. "Will it hold?" he asked. "The building, I mean?"

"It'll hold," Mara said. "Just keep moving."

The group moved, two floors down as instructed. On the second landing, Mara let herself take three controlled breaths while they shuffled past her. The kind of breaths she took behind the bar when the line got mean. Working rest. Then she moved again.

Mara opened the door at the base of the stairs a crack and checked the air: cool, sharp with disinfectant, but clear of smoke.

She turned to the trio. "Go left, past the elevators. You'll see Security and a path out."

The woman looked at her, eyes wide. "Are you coming?"

"I need to go back up," Mara said.

The woman shook her head. "That's insane."

"Yeah," Mara said, and almost smiled.

They went, half-running. Mara watched until they'd rounded the corner and were gone.

Then she turned back to the stairs, wiped her face with her sleeve, and started climbing.

***

In the GSOC, the floor map flickered and repopulated.

Red nodes bloomed across fourteen and fifteen, then bled downward as access badge readers failed in sequence, trapping people. Stairwells lit, went dark, lit again. Motion sensors tripped and retripped, stacking alerts faster than the system could clear them.

"Evacuation flow is off pattern," an operator said, voice tight. "We've got movement against protocol. People are exiting through service corridors."

"Hold," Maddy said. She stood behind the row of consoles, tablet in hand, eyes fixed on the map. "We haven't authorized a full override."

"Smoke's visible on multiple floors," the operator said. "If we unlock the east stack—"

"We don't unlock based on assumption," Maddy said. "We unlock based on confirmation."

Rick's voice cut in from the far console. "What's the confirmation delay?" No one moved until Maddy nodded.

"Fire panel data is corrupted," Maddy replied. "Alarm state is unstable. We don't know if this is a cascading fault or a contained electrical event."

"People are moving anyway," another operator said. "Someone's directing them."

Maddy tapped her screen. "Log unauthorized movement. Timestamp it. Capture camera angles on the west service stairs."

Rick turned in his chair. "Maddy, if they're already evacuating-"

"If we override without verification and someone is injured in a locked zone," Maddy said calmly, "that liability comes back to us. Procedure exists for a reason."

On the main screen, a cluster of blue dots shifted direction, funneling down a stairwell that wasn't on the approved evacuation map.

"That route isn't sanctioned," an operator said.

Maddy nodded once. "Exactly."

The alarms stuttered again. Three short bursts. Silence.

Rick swore under his breath. "We need to open the stack."

Maddy didn't move. "We need to document deviation first."

"People are in there," Rick said.

"And they're leaving," Maddy replied. "Which means the system isn't preventing egress. That distinction matters."

A new alert popped. ACCESS BADGE FAILURE: EAST CORE. Another followed it. DOOR STATUS UNKNOWN.

Maddy took a screenshot.

"Start an incident packet," she said. "This will require review."

Rick stared at the map, jaw tight, watching the unauthorized path stabilize into a steady flow.

"Someone's making decisions on the ground," he said.

"Yes," Maddy said. "And I want a clean frame. Face, badge sleeve, timestamp. If this turns into a legend, we'll have proof of the person who started it."

She tapped one more command, isolating the feed to the service stairwell.

"Keep recording," Maddy said. "If it repeats, it becomes a pattern."

***

Two floors up, Mara heard the pounding.

The steady kind. A rhythm of denial turning into panic.

She followed it down a short corridor and found a glass conference room sealed behind an access-controlled door. A dozen analysts crowded inside, faces washed pale by their laptop screens. They had piled chairs against the glass as if furniture could argue with a lock.

One of them saw her and pointed, mouth wide, voice lost to the alarm's broken warble.

Mara tried the reader. Dead. The little screen was blank, as if it had decided the room no longer existed.

Inside, someone slapped the glass again and held up a phone, screen bright with an error message. No signal. No instructions. Only smoke beginning to curl along the ceiling tiles.

Mara glanced down the hall and spotted the fire extinguisher cabinet. It was mounted on her side of the glass door, bright red and clean, useless to the people trapped behind glass.

The analysts saw it too. Their relief lasted half a second before they realized they couldn't reach it.

Mara pulled the extinguisher free, hefted its weight, and stepped back once.

The first strike spiderwebbed the glass. The sound snapped through the corridor like a gunshot. The people inside flinched, then surged forward.

Mara struck again, lower this time, widening the fracture. The panel slumped inward, still held together by its own film.

"Back up," she said. Final.

They obeyed. They were desperate, not stupid.

She swung the extinguisher again and again until the glass finally gave, collapsing in a glittering sheet. The analysts shrank back, arms up.

Everyone spilled out.

"Stairs," Mara said. "Down. Now!"

A man in a blue button-down blinked at her like he was trying to place her in his world. "Who are you?"

"I'm getting you out," Mara said. Her voice scraped. "Move!"

As they surged past her, someone whispered, almost hopeful, "It's the Phantom."

They poured out in a clumsy wave, coughing, eyes streaming. Mara pointed them toward the stairwell and stayed long enough to count heads, because that was the job now.

Then she turned and kept climbing.

The alarms were quieter on this side, almost gentle, like a lullaby sung from another room. Mara took the stairs two at a time only on the way up, using the rail to pull herself forward when her legs lagged. Her calves started to tremble on the landings, a warning her body kept issuing even when her head refused to listen.

She passed four floors before she heard another voice, a real human voice. It echoed from a corridor above, panicked, pleading.

She didn't stop at the sound itself. Not yet.

Voices carried in this building. Panic bounced off glass and concrete and traveled farther than people did. If she stopped for every echo, she'd lose the source.

She stopped on the next floor. The correct one.

A woman was crouched against the wall outside a supply room, arms wrapped around her head, breath coming in sharp gasps. Smoke hugged the ceiling above her, thin but creeping.

Mara dropped beside her. "Look at me."

The woman shook her head, sobbing.

"Look at me," Mara said again, louder. "You're not trapped. You can move."

The woman's eyes snapped up, wild.

"Can you stand?" Mara asked softly.

A nod. Barely.

Mara hauled her up, kept a hand on her elbow, and turned her toward the stairs. "Down," she said. "Both hands on the rail. Don't stop until the air changes."

"What about—"

"Later," Mara interrupted. "Go."

The woman stumbled, then found the rhythm of the steps and disappeared downward.

Mara waited three seconds. Long enough to be sure.

Then she turned and kept climbing.

At the next landing, she found another slumped against the wall: a custodian, older, eyes glazed, a dust mask pulled halfway off his chin. She checked his pulse. Strong, just knocked out by the air. She tried to rouse him with a slap, then shook him until his eyes fluttered open.

He saw her, looked confused, then groaned.

"Can you walk?" Mara asked.

The man nodded, weak, then struggled to stand. She got him upright, slung his arm over her shoulder, and guided him toward the service stairs. The alarms were dead here, the only sound the distant whine of HVAC trying and failing to compensate.

They descended together, slower than before. The man coughed, spat on the concrete, then found his stride.

"Almost there," Mara said, and this time she meant it.

At the ground level, she shouldered open the loading dock door and pushed him into daylight. Cool air hit them both at once, sharp and clean compared to the smoke inside.

The dock was crowded now. People she'd already routed out stood in small, shaken clusters, wrapped in borrowed coats and emergency blankets, faces turned back toward the building. A few looked up when the door opened.

The man staggered, then caught himself. Someone rushed forward to grab his arm.

Mara didn't stay. She turned back toward the door.

"Wait," the man said, hoarse.

She paused just long enough to look at him. "There are more people inside," she said.

As she stepped back inside, a sound followed her. Just a burst of applause, uneven and startled, mixed with a few shouts that didn't know what to say.

Somewhere in it, someone tried the name, half-laughing, half-disbelieving.

"See, it's the Phantom—"

The door swung shut before she heard the rest.

Mara took one breath, braced herself, and started up again.

At every landing, the smoke was thicker, the air hotter, the alarms less certain. Mara kept her mouth covered when she could, but her throat was raw now, and every inhale tasted like insulation.

She climbed until the numbers blurred, retracing floors she'd already cleared.

She stopped only once, at a small window on seventeen, and pressed her palm against the glass. To steal ten seconds of stillness.

Below, the plaza and garden were lit in hard flashes: emergency lights, headlights, the slow sweep of spot beams across glass. People clustered behind barricades in tight, dark knots. From this height, it all looked orderly, almost calm, like the Tower was still pretending it could contain itself.

Her reflection in the glass was almost unrecognizable. Soot-smeared. Eyes rimmed red. Hair pasted to her scalp.

When she peeled her hand away, her fingertips shook. She pressed them into a fist until the tremor stopped.

She was tired in a deep, boring way, the kind she'd learned to carry behind the bar. Twenty years on her feet had built something stubborn in her body. Panic gave it speed, but it didn't give it mercy.

She turned from the window and kept going.

Two floors later, a stairwell door buckled under heat and the landing filled with shouting. Mara listened for ten seconds and made the call she always made when the Tower stopped behaving.

She traced the noise to the stairwell on the east face, the nice side, where the access badge readers were supposed to be next-gen but hadn't been updated since rollout.

She opened the door, and the world filled with noise: a dozen people crammed onto the landing, one of them pounding the next door with a shoe. Two were crying, one hyperventilating into a brown paper lunch sack, another kneeling to help a woman who looked ready to faint. At the front, a man in a suit jacket torn at the elbow kept gesturing at the blocked exit, voice thick with panic.

Mara stepped in, hands raised. "This way," she said, but nobody heard over the shouting.

She repeated, louder. "This way!"

The man with the torn jacket turned around. "Are you kidding? There's smoke out there!"

Mara locked eyes with him, steady. "It's better than burning alive in a stairwell. The next landing's blocked. That door's hot, right?"

He blinked, unsure, then nodded.

She moved past him, straight to the woman kneeling with the other. "Can she walk?" Mara asked.

"She twisted her ankle," said the woman, voice trembling. "She can barely move."

Mara knelt beside the injured woman, saw the swelling, the heels already kicked off. She looked up at the two men. "You two. Get her under the arms. We're moving. Service stairs."

The group looked at each other, hope and disbelief flickering across their faces in equal measure.

"There's smoke up there," someone said.

"Better air on the other side," Mara replied. "Less risk. Trust me."

A cleaner in Facilities blue at the rear spoke up. "She's right. The service stairs breathe better."

Mara nodded her thanks, then turned back to the group. "We have to move. If we wait any longer, we're done."

The two men took the injured woman's shoulders and got her upright. The woman hissed in pain but let herself be hauled. The Facilities guy moved in to brace her other side.

"Stay together," Mara told the rest. "No running, no splitting off."

The man in the torn jacket hesitated, then took point, his earlier bravado curdling into something more useful. "Let's go," he said, rallying the rest.

Mara led them out to the stairwell, the group collapsing into a line, hands on the shoulder of the person in front. The smoke was denser now, but the ceiling height gave it space, and the emergency lights cast weird looping shadows.

The first obstacle was a cluster of boxes stacked to chest level, each labeled with a date and a five-digit code. Mara shoved them aside, creating a gap just wide enough for the group to snake through.

"Watch your step," she called back, and they navigated the mess, sneakers crunching glass and debris.

Halfway down the second flight, the injured woman started to falter. "I can't," she whispered, legs buckling.

"Yes, you can," Mara said, hoisting her higher. "Almost there."

The Facilities guy grunted under the weight but didn't slow.

Behind them, someone coughed hard, then spat. "It's getting worse," said a voice near the rear.

"Thirty feet," Mara said. "Then we're clear."

They made the final push to the seventh floor, opened the door, and entered the landing between elevators. The air was instantly better; still tense, but no longer acrid.

"Rest a minute here," Mara said, easing the injured woman to the floor. The others collapsed beside her, faces slick with sweat, every one of them breathing hard.

The man in the torn jacket looked up at Mara. "How did you know that would work?"

"I guessed," Mara said. "Sometimes the Tower helps. Sometimes it doesn't."

The Facilities guy grinned. "You sound like Janis."

Mara almost smiled at that.

She turned to the group. "You've got to keep moving. Take the stairs to the second floor, then go down the hall, then take the service stairs to the loading dock. You'll be safe there. Stay low. Cover your mouth if it gets worse."

They nodded, skepticism burned away by exhaustion and gratitude.

The injured woman met Mara's gaze, voice hoarse. "Are you coming?"

"Not yet," Mara said.

The Facilities guy shook his head. "You're nuts. But thanks."

"See you outside," Mara said, already moving back the way they'd come.

***

The seventh floor was no longer her secret.

By the time the next wave reached it, the bypass had become rumor, then plan. People arrived in clusters with soot on their sleeves and panic in their eyes, already repeating instructions they'd heard from someone else.

Mara didn't walk them out anymore. She turned them into a line and turned the line into a system.

"Listen," she said, voice sharp enough to cut through the noise. "You're going down. Now."

A man in a cardigan started to speak.

Mara pointed. "You. Front. Keep them together. If someone stops, you move them. If you get turned around, you follow the green tape and exit signs. You don't go looking for a better route. There is no better route."

He blinked like he wanted to argue, then nodded.

"Good." Mara pointed at the next person, a woman with steady eyes and a torn sleeve. "You stay in the back. Count heads. If someone drops, you tell the front, and you keep the line moving."

The woman nodded, jaw tight.

Mara pointed at the stairwell. "Go."

They went.

The next group surged in behind them, louder and less controlled. Two guys from Legal, an IT kid who looked too young to be here, and three people with phones out like screens could save them.

"Put the phones away," Mara said. "Light if you need it, but no recording. Move."

Someone tried to ask about the alarms.

"They're not coming back," Mara said. Her voice scraped. "Besides, we already know there's a fire. Stairs. Down."

This time she didn't wait for agreement. She took the IT kid by the shoulder, turned him toward the stairwell, and pushed him into motion. The rest followed because people followed movement.

Across the corridor, a rolling bin scraped into view. Janis appeared with a mask over her mouth and blue tape wrapped down one forearm like she'd marked herself for the job.

"You're making good time," Janis said.

"Not good enough," Mara replied. "The east core is gone. We lost landings."

Janis jammed a wedge under a door without looking. "West stairs are still open, but Security tried to block them. They're only letting the top floors through."

Mara didn't ask how she knew. She pointed at a darker corridor that ran parallel to the main hall. "We use the service cut-through."

Janis nodded. "I'll hold this door. You keep them moving."

The next wave passed between them, heads down, shirts pulled up over noses. Someone tried to thank Janis.

Janis waved them away. "Save it for outside."

Mara picked two steady people in the group.

"You two. Front and back. You keep them moving. If you get stuck, you take the next stairwell down and don't come back up."

They nodded without hesitation, grateful for an order that made sense.

The reader on the next door was dead, but the latch was still physical. Mara put her shoulder into the bar and forced it open. Cooler air moved downward.

"All the way down," she told them. "No stops. If you get turned around, you follow the green tape."

That was enough. The group moved.

Mara watched them disappear down the stairs. Then she turned back toward the bypass corridor.

It was crowded now, several groups converging at once. Even panicked, they kept reaching for rank, as if the Tower had an executive escape route for emergencies.

Mara stepped between them and raised her voice.

"You all want out, you take the west stairs," she said. "If you can't walk, you get help now. Phones are lights only. Point them at the floor."

The arguing stopped. The groups reorganized around her words because her words were a plan they didn't have.

Someone asked, "What about the upper floors. Isn't anyone coming for them?"

Mara shook her head once. "Not yet. We do this ourselves. Move."

Janis secured carts against a door to keep it from closing. Then she gave Mara a hand signal. Two fingers, then a fist, then a point upward.

Two floors up. Problem above.

Mara nodded and pointed at a man with broad shoulders and an intact jacket. "You. You're leading this group down. Don't stop at the lobby. You go to the loading dock. Stay with them."

He opened his mouth, then closed it and nodded.

Mara turned and climbed.

On the ninth-floor landing, she found Sammy at an electrical panel, prying at it with a screwdriver. Soot streaked his sleeves. His hands were steady anyway.

"You good?" Mara asked.

Sammy glanced up and grinned like he hated the question. "Define good."

"Alive. Still working."

Sammy nodded. "I bypassed the locks on the next two floors. But ten is pulling smoke like a chimney. You'll have to crawl it."

Mara didn't argue. "How long?"

"Thirty seconds if you know the vents," Sammy said. "Longer than that and you'll pass out."

She looked down the corridor, then back to him. "You coming?"

He shook his head. "If I leave this panel, the odd floors lose air."

Mara accepted it. "Yell if you need backup."

Sammy's smile didn't reach his eyes. "You'll hear me."

Mara turned to the evacuees clustered behind her. Two techs and an HR woman she'd seen a hundred times in the café line. None of them looked ready.

"We go low," Mara said. "Fast. No talking. Follow my shoes."

The HR woman shook her head. "I'm not a runner."

"Neither am I," Mara said. "We're going anyway."

She cracked the door. Heat rolled out. Smoke hugged the ceiling. Mara dropped to hands and knees and moved, one hand over her mouth, the other feeling for obstacles. The group followed, coughing and whimpering, but they followed.

Halfway through, the lights died. For a second, the dark felt total.

Then a small LED beam cut forward. One of the techs, keychain light. Tiny, steady, enough.

At the far end, Mara hit the crash bar and the stairwell opened. Cleaner air pushed in. Survivable, at least. The group stumbled through, blinking, coughing, upright.

Mara counted heads. All accounted for.

"We made it?" the HR woman asked.

"Almost," Mara said. "Down one more level. Then you keep going until you get outside."

They moved.

At the bypass level, Janis was taping another wedge in place. She grinned when she saw Mara.

"Knew you'd show up," Janis said.

"Sammy's upstairs," Mara said. "He's keeping air on the odds."

"I'll make a pass after this round," Janis said, then looked at the evacuees. "You all know the way?"

They nodded. Janis waved them on.

Mara watched Janis work for one second.

"You always like this kind of chaos?" Mara asked.

Janis shrugged. "It's the only time they need us."

Mara didn't disagree. She was already turning back toward the stairs.

On what felt like her hundredth pass through the bypass, Mara noticed the change. People were looking for her.

"That's her," someone whispered.

"They said she'd be here," another voice answered.

A man in Security gear, face gray with smoke and exhaustion, stared at her as she passed. "You're the one from the café, right?"

Mara shrugged without slowing. "I just know the Tower."

"Whoever you are, keep doing what you're doing," the officer said. "It's working."

Mara didn't answer. She was already climbing again.

A man in a suit grabbed her arm near a stairwell landing, desperate enough to touch a stranger. "My wife is on nineteen. They told me to find you."

Mara didn't hesitate. "Wait at the west exit. I'll bring her down."

He let go, shaking, and Mara started up again, two stairs at a time.

Her calves trembled at the landing. She ignored it. She didn't negotiate with her body. Not yet.

By now, the legend moved ahead of her. People cleared a path when she came through. A woman lifted her phone, snapped a picture, then lowered it as if she were ashamed.

"She's real," the woman said, almost to herself.

Mara didn't care about being real. She cared about people getting out.

On nineteen, she found the wife. Soot on her face. Eyes sharp and unbroken. Two others huddled with her, stunned into stillness.

"We go now," Mara said.

They went. Single file. No arguing. No questions.

Down on the service level, the man was waiting. He hugged his wife hard enough to make her wince, then held her anyway. The two others vanished into the crowd outside, where survivors clustered behind tape and emergency lights and the hard glitter of glass.

Mara stood at the edge of the doorway and looked back at the Tower. The alarms still blared, softer now. The building groaned around the sound, as if it was getting tired too.

She could have stopped. She could have let the myth take over and vanish the way she always had.

Instead, she turned and walked back inside. Cheers radiated all around her.

She had the upper floors to clear.

CHAPTER EIGHTEEN

ELEANOR

By the time Mara reached the upper thirties, her body had started making decisions without asking her.

Her calves trembled every time she shifted her weight. Her knees burned hot and dull, the pain no longer sharp enough to warn her, just constant. Each breath came shallow and fast, like her lungs had forgotten how to fill all the way. The air tasted metallic, layered with plastic.

She kept climbing.

She couldn't stop wondering who might still be waiting.

By forty-eight, her legs were shaking so hard she had to pause with her forehead against the rail, counting until the stairwell stopped tilting.

Someone could still be alive.

That was enough.

She pushed on.

Above forty-eight, the Tower stopped pretending to be an office building.

The stairwell opened straight into the executive space.

Mara stopped just past the door.

The forty-ninth-floor corridor was quieter than it should have been. Smoke hung in loose bands near the ceiling, still.

Her legs trembled.

She told herself she would rest for ten seconds. Long enough to decide if this was where she stopped. She closed her eyes, her breathing slowed.

"Mara Flores!"

The voice cut through the haze like a hand closing around her throat. Clean. Controlled. The kind that expected doors to open.

Mara froze.

Nobody up here should have known her. Nobody up here should have been here at all.

"Mara, over here!"

Eleanor stood half inside a corner office, one hand braced against the doorframe. Two grandchildren huddled close in visitor lanyards, faces streaked with soot, and an older woman gripped the back of a chair like it was the only solid thing left in the world.

For a heartbeat, Mara just stared.

Then her instincts took over. They always did.

"You can walk?" Mara asked, already scanning the corridor, the vents, the ceiling.

"Yes," Eleanor said. "Not fast."

"That's fine," Mara said. "We just need steady."

Eleanor glanced at the stairwell, then back at Mara. "I don't know which routes are still open," she said. "You do."

"Then follow me."

They turned toward the stairs. Mara took point out of habit, then felt her leg give a warning tremor and adjusted, slowing just enough to keep them together.

Eleanor fell in beside her without being asked. Matching her pace.

"You don't look well," Eleanor said quietly.

"I'm fine," Mara said, and they both knew it wasn't true.

They started down.

By thirty-five, Mara's breathing had turned ragged. By twenty-five, her vision narrowed at the edges. Eleanor noticed the shift and slid an arm under Mara's elbow, taking weight without making a scene.

Mara let her.

They made it to nineteen before they heard the boots.

Firefighters, moving up fast, masks on, radios crackling.

One of them stopped short when he saw Eleanor. Another looked past her, clocked Mara's face, the soot.

"We've got you," he said. "Keep coming down."

Mara shook her head. "There might be more above."

"We'll handle it," he said, sharper now. "You did your part."

Mara started to turn upward.

Eleanor's hand closed around her waist.

"Mara!"

The way she said it was recognition. Like Mara was a person, not a rumor.

"How do you know my name?" Mara asked, breath breaking around the words.

Eleanor didn't stop walking. "I helped Andrea get the job in the GSOC."

The stairs blurred even more.

"Andrea?" Mara echoed.

Eleanor glanced down, just once, at the access badge clipped crookedly to Mara's jacket: A. Morales.

"I met her at the women's shelter where I volunteer," Eleanor said. "She was sharp. Quiet. Watching everything."

Mara swallowed, more smoke than air.

"She started in the GSOC," Eleanor said. "Worked her way up. Smart enough to scare people."

Eleanor kept her voice level, but her hand tightened on the rail. "She found the lie."

"Not a bad access badge scan. A bad building. Cheaper parts, signed off like they were the real thing."

"The garden," Mara said. "I found it in the garden."

"The garden?" Eleanor repeated, thinking. "Maybe she lost it. Maybe she lost it on purpose, for the next person."

Mara's grip tightened on the rail. "And I found it."

Eleanor didn't answer. She didn't need to.

They reached the next landing. The firefighters took the children and the older woman with gentle efficiency and started guiding them down.

Eleanor kept talking, voice steady, as if explaining it cleanly could make it make sense.

Mara listened for a few steps.

Then she heard it again, faint above the failing alarms. A cough. A voice. Not theirs.

She stopped at the landing.

Eleanor took about ten more steps before she felt the absence behind her. She turned, still mid-sentence.

Mara was already backing up the stairs, one hand on the rail, disappearing into the haze.

"Mara!" Eleanor called, and this time it sounded like panic.

A firefighter caught Eleanor's elbow. "Ma'am. Keep moving."

Eleanor fought the pull for one second too long, eyes fixed upward.

"Mara Flores!" she called.

The stairwell gave her only an echo.

CHAPTER NINETEEN

THE RETURN

From the stairwell window above the lobby, Mara watched the latest group of evacuees push through the glass doors. The crowd split and re-formed around the paramedics' station, a moving knot of blankets, soot, and stunned faces. Eleanor and the kids vanished into it. The older woman who had been with them let herself be guided away by an unfamiliar hand holding gauze.

Mara held still on the landing, arms crossed, invisible until the moment she chose to move.

Below, the lobby churned. Above it, the Tower had gone quiet.

The smoke didn't drift down. It thickened and settled, pooling along the ceiling in slow, oily bands. The air grew heavier with each minute. Somewhere, alarms had run out of power and degraded into a slow, funereal beep. The rest was the hush of wet concrete and tired systems.

She could have left. The path out was clear, at least for now.

Mara looked once toward the stairs.

Then she turned and climbed.

The ascent hurt immediately. Every landing felt different. Cold, then hot. Dry, then slick. The stairwell walls sweated, condensation cutting clean lines through the carbon smudges left by panicked hands. Halfway to three, her lungs burned hard enough to make her stop. She pressed her wrist to her mouth until the coughing eased.

At four, a child's handprint pressed on the wall. Mara stepped around it and kept going.

She heard a scream. Barely audible. Almost nothing.

She stopped, counted to three, and heard it again. Higher this time. Real.

She climbed faster, hands on the rail, shoes slipping once on damp concrete. At six, the door opened onto heat and a blue-gray haze.

The landing was packed with people, five or six, sealed behind an access-controlled glass fire door. The handle on Mara's side was blackened. Untouchable. The access badge reader glowed red instead of green.

A woman in an ill-fitting pantsuit and no shoes pounded the glass with both fists from the other side. Behind her, a Facilities cleaner knelt with his head between his knees, arms locked around himself to keep from shaking.

"Don't touch that handle," Mara said, flat and loud. "It'll cook you."

They startled. The woman's eyes flicked to Mara, then away, as if hope itself were dangerous.

"It won't open," the woman gasped. "The reader's dead. The other stairwell's full of smoke."

"It's fried," Mara said.

She leaned closer to the glass and raised her voice. "You. Find a heavy chair. Metal if you can. Aim for the corner, not the middle."

The woman stared at her like she'd suggested jumping.

"Now!" Mara said. "Corner. Low."

One of the men vanished into the haze and came back dragging a heavy chair, its legs scraping the floor. He raised it like he didn't believe in what he was about to do.

"Low," Mara said again. "Hard."

The first hit starred the glass. It held, webbed, stubborn. The second strike deepened the cracks, the wire inside whining as it strained. The third blow punched a jagged opening through and the pane sagged inward in a slow collapse of shards and mesh.

"Back," Mara said.

They flinched away as the last of the glass gave. Mara stepped through the gap without touching the frame and grabbed the woman by the sleeve, pulling her clear of the broken edge.

The cleaner lifted his head. "The air's solid. We'll suffocate."

Mara ignored him. "Now. You two, get him up."

She pointed at the two nearest men, then at the woman in the pantsuit. "You count heads. Every ten steps."

They moved because her voice gave them something else to do.

Behind Mara, something cracked overhead. A ceiling tile dropped, then another, and the stairwell filled with dust and hot grit. The rail vibrated under her palm, a shudder that ran downward like a warning.

Mara didn't look back.

"This stair's a death trap," she said. "We take the copy rooms and cut west. Stay low."

Mara forced the office door open with her sleeve wrapped tight around her hand. Smoke rolled out. She shoved it forward with her forearm and ducked inside, motioning the rest through.

The air in the copy room was barely better. Printers sat dead but blinking. Paper stuck to the floor in damp sheets. Mara crossed to the far door and tested the knob. Warm, but not hot. She braced and forced it open.

"Out," she said. "Single file."

They followed, stumbling, counting under their breath.

Down the corridor, lights blinked and died. An exit sign flickered green at the far end.

At the cross corridor, Mara listened, then knocked hard on the next door. It opened a crack.

Inside were three more. A man in a gray blazer, an older woman with lipstick smeared down her chin, and a boy in an orange hoodie.

"There's a group down the hall," Mara said. "Get with them. Don't look back."

"Who are you?" the man asked.

"Follow the voice," Mara said. "Move."

The boy stared at her. "You're the ghost."

Mara didn't answer. She turned and kept them moving.

They regrouped. Nine now. The cleaner groaning but upright.

The next junction was blocked by furniture stacked nearly to the ceiling. Desks, chairs, and a metal filing cabinet.

"Up and over," Mara said. "If you fall, crawl forward."

They climbed. She hauled. She directed. She didn't let anyone stop.

At the far end, another glass access door.

Heat surged. Smoke thickened.

Mara turned. "You," she said to the younger tech. "Grab the small metal filing cabinet."

He hesitated.

"Now!" she snapped.

He ran and came back with the cabinet, hands burned raw.

"Low," Mara said. "Aim for the corner."

The first strike starred the glass. The second blew it inward.

"Back."

Cooler air rushed through.

They poured into the stairwell. Mara counted heads. All of them.

She leaned against the wall and let the coughing take her, then waved them on.

She waited until the last footsteps faded before she moved again.

There were still floors above.

She turned back into the smoke.

Mara vanished into it the way she always had, without waiting to be seen.

***

Elsewhere in the Tower, Janis was doing one last sweep because nobody had told her to stop.

She called it habit. She checked the west bypass, the service cut-through, and the places people got stuck when they stopped thinking. In a building like this, the map never mattered as much as the choke points.

The west bypass was clear. The service cut-through was holding. People were still moving, quieter now. Controlled. They moved in lines, heads down, hands on rails, following tape and rumor and whatever voice had last told them what to do.

Janis followed the flow until it thinned.

At the end of the corridor, a door stood half open that should have been shut.

It wasn't one of the doors people used. No signage. No reason for it to be open. The kind of door you passed for years without noticing, until it became the only one that mattered.

Janis frowned and stepped closer.

The door was already open, held on a narrow gap that should have snapped shut. Heat breathed through the opening. Stale warmth.

Janis put her hand on the edge and felt it tremble, not from movement, from pressure in the frame. The door wanted to close. Something was stopping it.

She leaned in, careful, using her shoulder to keep the gap from shrinking.

Something shifted on the other side with a dull scrape.

The door sagged inward a fraction, and a body slid with it, catching on the threshold before dropping.

For a second, Janis didn't move.

Her mind tried to label it as anything else. A fallen coat. A bag. A piece of furniture dragged into place. Anything except what it was.

Then she saw the hand.

One arm stretched toward the latch, fingers curled like they'd been holding on. The knuckles were black with soot. The skin looked wrong, too dry, too still.

Janis dropped to her knees.

"Mara," she said, but it came out as air, not a name.

Mara lay against the frame, head turned slightly toward the crack of daylight. Her face was smeared and blackened. Her hair stuck to her cheek in wet strands. Her chest didn't move.

Janis put two fingers to Mara's neck anyway.

Nothing.

Behind Janis, footsteps. Coughs. Someone stumbling.

"Keep moving," Janis said, voice low and hard. "Don't stop here."

A shadow fell across the doorway as several evacuees reached the corridor, saw Janis on the floor, saw the shape at her knees, and froze.

"Move!" Janis repeated.

They obeyed, slipping past through the opening.

Janis looked at the door. Looked at the angle of it.

Then she understood.

Mara hadn't been lying there.

Mara had been the wedge.

Her weight had held the door just far enough open to keep the latch from catching, just far enough to keep air moving, just far enough for a line of people to keep slipping through.

Janis swallowed hard, and her throat made a sound that was almost a sob.

Of course.

Of course, Mara would do it that way.

Not dramatic. Not visible. Just necessary.

A man shoved through the doorway, coughing so hard he nearly folded. His leg brushed Mara's shin as he passed. Janis flinched, then forced herself still.

The line mattered more than her feelings. Mara would have demanded that.

Janis shifted her body carefully and pulled Mara's arm back from the hinge so it wouldn't get caught as more people passed. She didn't move her far. She didn't change the shape of her. She just kept the door open and kept Mara from getting dragged.

People kept coming. Two, then three, then a small cluster. Their eyes slid over Mara and away again, not because they didn't care, because the building didn't give them room to.

Janis stayed on her knees with one hand on the door and one hand on Mara's sleeve, holding both in place.

When the last of them stumbled through and the corridor finally went quiet, Janis didn't stand.

She leaned forward until her forehead touched Mara's shoulder. The fabric was stiff with soot. Still warm, like the heat hadn't decided what belonged to the living.

Janis kept her voice low, like they were at the café before dawn.

"You did enough," she said. "You did plenty."

Footsteps returned. Boots. Radios.

A firefighter stopped short, took in the door, the corridor, Janis on the floor.

He looked at Mara and went still.

Janis didn't look up. "Don't close it," she said. "It'll catch."

The firefighter nodded once and braced the door with his shoulder. Another moved past and checked the corridor beyond. A third crouched, careful, and checked Mara's pulse as if the ritual mattered.

He looked at Janis and shook his head.

Janis already knew.

She stayed there until someone put a hand on her elbow and said her name.

She stood slowly, knees protesting, and stepped aside as they lifted Mara with the same gentle efficiency they used on the living.

Janis watched them carry her away through the corridor she'd kept clean for years.

The door, freed of weight, tried to swing shut.

Janis caught it and held it open until they were clear.

Only then did she let it close.

Later, they said the routes held. The west bypass stayed open long enough. The service cut-through stayed clear long enough. People made it out in lines.

They would say the building fought itself and lost.

They would say the Phantom kept the paths open.

Janis didn't argue.

The door stayed open long enough. That was what Mara had done.

CHAPTER TWENTY

ASH AND AFTERMATH

The emergency blanket clung to Marcy's shoulders, static popping on every breath, and the orange mesh left a grid pattern on her arms that she couldn't scrub off. She sat on an upended water cooler, knees tucked tight, lips stained blue from a trauma kit, and she watched the triage tent like a game show she didn't remember auditioning for.

Every few minutes, a new round of victims. Some walking. Some rolled in on cots. Some just deposited and left, limbs askew. The paramedics moved like a pit crew, triaging by color, banding wrists and moving on. Marcy coughed once, shallow and embarrassed, the kind of cough you did when you wanted the world to see you were still in it.

Next to her, a man with a ruptured nose pressed a bag of ice to his face and groaned. Beyond him, a woman in the world's least flattering suit skirt dabbed blood from her knees and tried to talk into a dead phone. The world was nothing but small piles of suffering.

Marcy didn't expect to see Mara. It was her day off.

Still, she scanned every face that came out, because Mara wasn't answering her phone.

She checked each new arrival, every bandaged head and tear-streaked face. She ran the inventory with barista precision. Hair, height, posture. Mara would stand out, even in a crowd this sad. Or maybe not, Marcy corrected herself. That was the point of Mara, wasn't it? Invisible until you needed her, then gone again before you had time to say thanks.

A young Security guard wandered by with a clipboard, stopped to look at his own hands like he'd forgotten what to do with them. Marcy watched him, amused, until he caught her eye and offered a weak "You holding up?" as if it were company policy.

"Sure," Marcy said, "if you consider not dead a win."

He didn't laugh, just nodded and kept walking.

Rumors moved faster than the boots did. A collapse on the upper floors. A group trapped behind an access badge door. A "woman from the café" who showed up like she'd been waiting for the worst moment.

Marcy heard that one twice. First, from a guy in Legal bleeding from both shins. Then, from a Facilities old-timer with soot in the lines of his face.

"Didn't get a good look," the Legal guy said, shaking his head. "Average height. Dark hair. Calm. Said she lived here."

Classic Mara. Showing up when you didn't want her to, and then refusing to take a bow.

But then the story shifted. It always did. Somebody else said the Phantom did it. The ghost in the walls. The one who wedged doors and moved through the building like it had been built for her. Someone swore the Phantom ran back inside after getting people out.

Marcy let the stories swirl and kept her own suspicions tucked behind her teeth. Mara would explain herself if she were out here.

But Mara wasn't out here.

Every few minutes, another wave spilled through the doors, wet with sweat or sprinkler runoff, faces smudged gray. Marcy scanned for the familiar silhouette, the careful way Mara held her head, the particular flatness in her eyes.

Nothing.

A woman from HR, Tricia, came out with a shock blanket over her head and collapsed into a squat by the curb. Marcy gave her a nod and got back a blank stare.

The Tower itself was a wound on the skyline, shivering behind smoke and steam. Fire crews ringed the base, aiming hoses up into the open mouth of the mezzanine. Security cordoned off the front with tape and authoritative shouting. Beyond it, a river of press and bystanders swelled against the barricades, faces turned up, waiting for collapse or for a miracle.

Marcy sat and watched, numbness taking root.

At some point, a volunteer pressed a water bottle into her hand and said, "Sip, don't chug."

Marcy did both, then wiped her mouth on the back of her wrist.

The man with the broken nose beside her was gone, replaced by a teenage girl in a blood-streaked company T-shirt who checked her phone every ten seconds.

"You got out okay," Marcy asked, voice low.

The girl blinked at her, startled. "Yeah. Some lady said take the west stair, so I did."

Marcy nodded, not sure what to say.

"I think the lady is still inside," the girl added, and her voice cracked. "She's smart though. She'll find a way."

Marcy wanted to say not everyone gets out. She kept it to herself. The girl was holding on to the only kind of hope left.

Marcy tried to piece together the last hour, the path she'd taken. The moment the lights died. The smell of burning plastic. The crush at the stairwell. The way her shoes slipped on wet tile. She remembered grabbing a stranger's hand and not letting go until they hit open air. She remembered thinking, at every turn, Mara would know what to do.

But Mara wasn't here.

An older man in a maintenance uniform limped out of the triage tent and stopped near Marcy like he'd been looking for her on purpose.

"You see Flores?" he asked.

Marcy's heart stuttered. "Who?"

"Flores. Mara."

"No," Marcy said. One word. Nothing else.

The man nodded, eyes heavy, and shuffled off.

Marcy turned, as if Mara might be standing behind her anyway. There was only the girl with the phone and a Security guard retching into the gutter.

Time passed. It always did. They loaded the worst off into ambulances, and the rest clustered in packs, shaking and alive and trying not to show it. Marcy listened as the stories began to solidify. Less rumor now. More myth. The woman from the café. The Phantom. The one who saved dozens, maybe even more, by knowing every back path, every trick of the Tower.

Marcy realized she'd stopped shivering. She ran a hand over her arm, felt the residue of soot and insulation, felt the lattice of the blanket pressed into her skin.

She looked up at the Tower, the top still hidden by smoke. She searched the crowd, then the sidewalk, then the sky.

Mara wasn't coming out.

The stories were all the same in the end. Someone goes in, saves the others, and disappears. The crowd moves on. The building gets repaired. The news cycle refreshes. But the story keeps circling, tight and unbreakable.

Marcy felt the hollow settle in her chest.

She thought about the way Mara used to talk about coffee, how you could always tell the good beans by what remained after the cup was gone.

She sat, wrapped in her blanket, and waited for the aftertaste.

It took its time.

***

The first time Janis Miller tried to leave the triage zone, a paramedic stopped her with two fingers to the shoulder and a look that said don't test me. Janis recognized the type. Twenty-five, still able to sprint in their gear, new authority stapled to their posture. She let them tape her wrist, shine a light in her eyes, and recite the same list of questions until they lost interest.

Then she pocketed the water bottle they offered and took the perimeter like she was casing a job.

From the outside, the scene was orderly. Corrals for the uninjured. The walking wounded lined up for wristbands. Security kept the media back with yellow tape and bored belligerence. Janis moved in slow arcs, scanning for someone and refusing to look like it mattered.

The third pass, she found Sammy.

He was hunched on the curb, hands dangling between his knees, a borrowed oxygen mask pressing his hair flat. His shirt was burned open at the collar and his hands were nicked to hell, but he didn't look scared.

Just tired.

"Sammy," Janis said, settling beside him with the careful grace of a woman who hated fuss.

He blinked at her through the plastic, recognition slow. "You made it."

"Yeah," Janis said. "You look like hell."

He grinned, or tried to, then lifted the mask. "I thought you were stuck on fourteen."

"Fourteen was a mess," Janis said. "Cut through the west stairwell and hit the garden before the smoke could catch up."

Sammy nodded, set the mask in his lap, and eyed the wound on his left knuckle. "Heard you were propping doors the whole way."

"They wouldn't hold otherwise," Janis said. "You know the hardware."

He smiled, which made his lips split and spot fresh blood on his chin. "You see Mara?"

Janis hesitated, the pause longer than she meant. "Not yet. Thought she'd be out by now."

Sammy's hands flexed in his lap. "She's not at triage."

"She'll turn up," Janis said, voice flat, like stating it could make it true.

They sat together and watched the sun hammer the pavement. Every so often, a Security officer with a clipboard shuffled past asking the same questions. Name. Floor. Anyone still missing?

"Was Mara Flores with you?" the officer asked.

Janis shook her head once. "She didn't come out."

The officer paused, then wrote faster.

"She was clearing the upper floors," Janis added. "Knew them better than anyone."

After a while, Janis stretched her legs, shaking numbness out. "I always figured it'd be the gas main," she said quietly. "Not the access badge readers."

Sammy's laugh came out as a wheeze. "Should've bet on both."

They shared that moment of grim satisfaction, then lapsed back into watching survivors stagger through the gauntlet. It wasn't just staff now. Families and executives mixed in. Some in shock. Some already fielding calls or filming statements for whatever crisis PR needed a face.

Janis spotted Charles Denham at the far edge, sleeves rolled, phone pressed to his head. His suit was clean, as if he'd stepped out of the fire and into a tailor's mirror.

Janis didn't care about him.

But the woman beside him, hair streaked with sweat, had the same composure Janis remembered from years of watching people walk through the lobby. Eleanor Sterling. She wasn't doing the comforting. She was directing the nurses, picking out strays and putting them in order with a calm that made Janis respect her.

"She's okay in my book," Sammy said, following Janis's gaze.

They watched Eleanor finish triage, then pull Charles aside for a private word. His shoulders hunched like he was bracing for a punch. Eleanor's face never changed. She looked past him, scanning the scene like she was hunting.

"She's looking for something," Sammy said.

"Someone," Janis corrected.

They both knew who.

A cluster of maintenance guys gathered by the water station, trading stories with the hush of survivors comparing notes. Janis and Sammy drifted over. Marcy arrived at the same time.

"She saved us," one of them said, hands shaking as he fumbled a protein bar. "If she hadn't gotten that door open..."

"She was on every floor," another said. "I don't even know how she got between them."

"Phantom," someone called out.

"I think so," said the first guy, voice rising. "She moved like she didn't get tired. I think her name started with an M..."

"Mara," said Janis, Marcy, and Sammy all at the same time, and the little circle went silent.

"Yeah," the guy said. "You know her?"

"Everyone knows Mara," Marcy said, and didn't say anything else.

"Last I saw, she was with Security, west stairs," Sammy said. "Anyone see her come out?"

The others shook their heads, shame blooming in the silence.

Janis didn't say anything.

Sammy watched her, then nodded, accepting the part nobody wanted to say out loud. "She's still in there, then."

"Yeah," Janis said. "She is."

They left the group. Comfort from strangers didn't help today.

On the far side of the parking lot, Eleanor was laying into Charles, voice low and precise. You couldn't hear words, but you could read the shape. A reaming. Janis admired the economy of it. Eleanor didn't waste energy on tears.

Charles wilted, then straightened like he'd decided something and walked toward the security line, toward reporters pressed against the tape. Eleanor watched him go, then scanned the triage tent again.

Janis caught her eye for a second. Recognition. Gratitude. A quick look away. Enough.

Near dusk, they came for statements.

Security first, then a man from HR who looked like he'd never seen sun before. He asked the time of exit, names of anyone they'd seen, whether anyone "failed to evacuate" when ordered.

Janis let Sammy do most of the talking. When they asked about Mara, he kept it tight.

"She was above us," Sammy said. "Last seen helping a group at sixteen. She knew every shortcut."

The HR man made a note, then asked, "You think she made it out?"

Janis stared him down. "If she had, she'd be standing right here."

The man didn't argue.

They waited for the final word anyway. That was what you did when your body refused to believe what your eyes had already seen.

***

It started with the email.

The language was precise. Final casualty list. Acknowledgments. Procedural deviations under review.

Janis didn't see a signature, but she recognized Maddy in the phrasing immediately. Passive voice where responsibility should have lived. Careful verbs. Nothing that admitted failure. Nothing that gave grief a place to land.

Mara Flores wasn't described as a rescuer.

She was described as operating outside assigned scope.

Worse, she wasn't described as missing.

She was described as a deviation.

Sammy Tran read it on his phone at the maintenance break table, coffee cooling beside his elbow, hands still stained from cleanup. The list ran twenty-three names. Most were familiar, at least in passing. Two from Legal. One from Procurement. One from HR. Six janitorial, the ones who'd stayed behind to hold doors and clear stairwells for strangers who wouldn't remember them.

At the bottom, like a closing argument:

Flores, Mara – Café.

He stared at the words until they stopped looking like language and started looking like a dare.

Across from him, Janis hunched over a bowl of oatmeal. She'd lost weight since the fire, cheekbones sharper, skin paler. She didn't ask about the email. She must have seen it already.

"They're not even doing a plaque," Sammy said, voice flat.

Janis shrugged. "Not until Legal's done. Nobody wants to admit the access badge upgrades killed more people than they saved."

Sammy tapped his fingers on the table, restless. "She's not even a person to them. Just a line in the report."

"She was always more alive than the suits upstairs," Janis said. She lifted a spoonful of oatmeal and set it down without tasting it. "Don't let the words mess with you. People remember what matters."

Sammy nodded, but didn't buy it. He watched the break room fill, the new cleaning crew moving like ghosts, all of them avoiding the wall where Mara used to pin the bad customer notes. Someone had taken down the poster of the Tower's opening day. Now there was only a smear of sticky tape and a chunk of peeled paint.

In the silence, Sammy imagined Mara's laugh.

He wondered if anyone else ever would.

***

Two floors up, Marcy worked the temporary café. She salvaged the espresso machine and set up a counter in the corner of the lobby with folding tables. The traffic was lighter now. Most of the tenants were still remote, many too spooked to return.

Marcy didn't care.

She had more time to perfect her latte art, which she now used exclusively to draw little ghosts on every cup.

Before the first customer, she filled a glass with water and slid in a handful of grocery-store flowers.

Nothing fancy.

A few stems bent at odd angles, petals already bruising at the edges.

She set the glass beside the espresso machine and adjusted it twice until it sat where it wouldn't get knocked over.

Then she wiped the counter in long, deliberate arcs, pushing every stray crumb into her palm the way Mara always did.

When she finished, the flowers looked like they had always belonged there.

She read the email on her phone, holding it at arm's length as if the words might bite her. When she got to Mara's name, a sound came out of her that wasn't a laugh or a sob. Something raw and animal.

A customer, one of the new Security guys, looked over, startled.

"You good?" he asked, like he was programmed to care.

Marcy wiped her nose with the back of her hand. "Never better," she said, then added, "You want your regular?"

The guard nodded, but kept his distance. Marcy made the coffee, drew a perfect wraith in the foam, and handed it over with a smile she didn't feel.

"They're saying you all had a real hero," the guard said cautiously. "Saved a ton of people. No one's talking about it, but…"

"Yeah," Marcy said. "We did."

She watched him leave, then poured herself a double shot, drank it neat, and stared at the empty space behind the counter where Mara used to stand. Sunlight through the new windows left a trapezoid of light on the floor, just the right size for two people to work side by side.

Marcy didn't let herself cry.

Mara would have hated that.

***

The first month was investigations. After that, repairs. Soon, people were pretending again.

The investigation was ugly. Hearings. Subpoenas. A day when the press came and swarmed the Tower with cameras and fake empathy. Rick Holman, once the last word in Security, now just another suit in a cheap clip-on tie, sat at the witness table and tried to explain his decisions.

They gave him every chance to shift blame, but Rick was too proud to duck. He spoke in the same clipped phrases he'd always used. We acted on the best available data. No prior incident indicated this level of risk. Chain of command followed to the letter.

But when they got to the access badge upgrades, the locked doors, the failed overrides, Rick hesitated.

The fire marshal didn't let it pass. "And the fire and life safety components," she said. "The doors, the seals, the cabling. Items your own security compliance analyst, Andrea Morales, flagged as nonconforming." She flipped to a marked exhibit. "Ms. Morales wrote the first memo six months before the fire."

A deafening silence moved through the room.

Rick's jaw tightened. The pause was a thousandth of a second, but everyone saw it.

The fire marshal leaned forward. "Is it true that, in the final hours, the main stairwell was inaccessible to occupants above the twelfth floor?"

Rick nodded. "Yes."

"And that, according to multiple survivors, an employee outside her 'assigned role' moved through restricted areas during the incident, by-passing access controls and guiding evacuees to safety."

Another nod. "Yes."

The fire marshal didn't smile. "And the name of this individual."

Rick looked down at the table. "Mara Flores."

"Would you like to amend your previous statement regarding her unauthorized access to secure areas?"

Rick closed his eyes. "She did the job none of us could."

There was no applause. No catharsis. Just the click of a stenographer's keys and the sense that Rick had finally accepted he was no longer in charge.

Afterwards, he found Janis outside the hearing room, hands jammed in his pockets.

"You did good work," Rick said, voice flat. "All of you."

Janis looked at him, eyes dry as sand. "Try telling the Tower that."

He tried to say more, but she was already gone.

***

Months went by. The media cycle spun, then moved on. The Tower's repairs were ahead of schedule. But the story kept growing, piece by piece.

In the new break room, someone started a sticky note wall. Every day, a new post.

Mara sighting on 18.

Who fixed the printer? It was probably Mara.

Stuck access badge again. Guess who fixed it?

Sammy saw it first, then added one of his own. Still the best coffee.

Even the new hires picked up the habit. At first, they treated it as a joke. Then it turned into a ritual. If the elevator jammed or the power blinked, someone would say, "She's still watching out for us."

Janis never added a note, but she smiled every time she passed the wall.

***

On a Friday night, after the last shift, Sammy stopped by the café. Marcy was closing up, wiping counters with long arcs. She looked up, saw Sammy, and gave him a real smile and a two-finger salute.

"You want a drink?" she asked.

He shook his head. "Just wanted to see the place."

She leaned on the counter, studied his face. "You ever think about leaving?"

"All the time," Sammy said. "But the building wouldn't let me."

Marcy laughed, and it sounded like it hurt. "Yeah. I get that."

They stood in silence, the hiss of the lights the only sound.

Finally, Sammy said, "You know what she'd say about all this?"

"What?" Marcy said as she smacked her gum.

He mimicked Mara's voice, flat and precise. "Some things only work if you don't let people see you sweating."

Marcy grinned, then wiped at her eyes with the back of her hand. "That's so Mara."

Sammy nodded and pushed a sticky note across the counter. It read: Don't forget the human override.

He turned and left without saying another word.

Marcy stuck the note to the wall at eye level, where everyone could see it.

She finished the close, counted the tips, and turned off the lights.

For a long time, she just stood in the dark, letting her eyes adjust, waiting for the aftertaste.

This time, it came quicker.

And it stayed.

Chapter Twenty-One

THE MEMORIAL

The lobby looked wrong, even six months after the fire.

The paint was fresh. The access badge readers were new. The LED strips burned too bright, like they were trying to make up for something.

The sound was what gave it away.

Marcy's shoes echoed longer than they should have.

Voices stopped too quickly, like people didn't trust the air to carry them.

The Tower was open, technically, but it didn't feel inhabited.

It felt staged.

She arrived early.

The memo had said grand reopening, but there were still cones by the elevators and scaffolding wrapped in plastic that breathed faintly when the HVAC kicked on.

Someone had stacked drywall near the entrance, half barricade, half warning.

Marcy went straight to the café.

The espresso machine was already warm. Flowers neatly displayed nearby.

That stopped her.

Mara always did that part. She used to say cold machines made bitter coffee, and bitter coffee made bitter people. Marcy stood there longer than she needed to, hands hovering, waiting for the rest of the routine to come back.

It didn't.

She reached for the grinder. Checked the dial. Too fine. She adjusted it automatically and waited for the voice that usually followed.

You're going to choke it.

Nothing.

She turned the grinder on anyway.

The sound was too loud in the empty lobby. It bounced up the glass and came back at her wrong.

Of course it did.

Today was the memorial.

Everyone knew it. You could see it in the way people moved, careful and deliberate, like they were walking through a room where someone might still be sleeping.

White folding chairs leaned against the garden entrance. A woman from HR hovered nearby, checking her watch, then checking it again.

Marcy lined up cups. Compostable. New. Printed with a small ghost logo, not the corporate seal. She turned them so the logos faced forward.

Without thinking, she set out two towels.

Then she stared at the extra one like it had betrayed her, folded it once, and slid it under the counter where nobody would see.

Facilities showed up first. They always did. Blue vests, scuffed boots, eyes trained on exits and floors and one another. One of them stopped at the counter and pointed at the pastry case.

"You knew her?"

"Yeah," Marcy said. "We worked together."

He nodded, satisfied, and ordered black coffee. No lid. No sugar. He left a tip that felt like an apology.

The lobby filled slowly. Survivors mixed with people who had only ever seen the fire on screens. Executives arrived in pairs, voices low, hands already rehearsing where to stand. Security drifted toward the walls, unsure whether they were on duty or attending.

Maddy stood near the back, just inside the line of Security, tablet tucked under her arm. Her jacket read GSOC SUPERVISOR in small stitched letters, new enough to look stiff. Rick's old pacing spot was hers now. She scanned the room the way she always did, counting clusters, noting who spoke to whom, already sorting the morning into categories that would survive review. Rick used to call it presence. Maddy called it control. Now that he was gone, the room belonged to her.

Sammy came in just before ten.

He didn't order. Just stood at the counter, hands in his pockets, staring at the ghost cups.

"Every shift," he said, when Marcy asked if he was okay.

She poured him coffee anyway. Her hands shook. She spilled a little on the saucer and wiped it off with her sleeve instead of starting over.

Mara would have noticed.

At ten-thirty, the new supervisor called her over for a quick check-in. Perfect smile. Clipboard he didn't need.

"Garden event at noon," he said. "Catering run. Keep it neat."

"Statue?" Marcy asked.

He hesitated. "A commemorative."

"Sure."

She filled the catering bins with the same precision she'd learned from Mara. Don't overstack. Don't rush. Don't forget the creamer even if nobody uses them.

She burned the first pot of coffee and dumped it without comment.

***

The garden was the only place in the Tower that still felt like outside. Glass walls. A fake creek bed. Ficus trimmed too perfectly. Water trickling through a channel no one ever looked at.

At the far end sat a shape under black cloth.

Marcy didn't look at it.

People gathered in careful clumps. Facilities together. Security together. Survivors together. Executives separate, as always.

Janis stood at the back, hands folded, staring at the floor like she was waiting for a call that wasn't coming. Sammy hovered near the edge, coffee cup cradled like it mattered.

Eleanor Sterling, CEO by catastrophe and board vote, didn't go to the mic. She stood near the covered bench, hands folded, face unreadable, as if she refused to turn grief into a presentation.

At noon, an HR woman stepped up to the microphone and began speaking in the voice reserved for lawsuits and funerals.

"We are gathered here—"

Marcy stopped listening.

She watched faces instead. The ones that nodded because they were supposed to. The ones that didn't. The ones that looked like they were hearing Mara's name for the first time and deciding whether they should feel ashamed about that.

Executives spoke next. Each one tried to make Mara sound like a product. A reflection of culture. A success story.

Marcy felt something hot and tight settle behind her ribs.

Charles Denham, the former CEO, took the mic last.

He didn't look at the crowd. Just the covered shape at the front of the room. And the crowd didn't look at him.

"Mara Flores worked in this building for twenty years," he said. "Most of us didn't know her name until the day she saved more lives than any system we ever built."

The room shifted. People leaned in without realizing they were doing it.

"She was quiet," Charles said. "But she knew this place. Every flaw. Every shortcut. And when the systems failed, she didn't."

He stopped there.

He stepped back from the microphone.

"Eleanor."

Eleanor didn't move at first.

Then she walked straight to the covered bench and stood there for a moment, hands folded, like she was waiting for permission that wasn't coming.

She pulled the cloth away.

The statue was just Mara.

Seated on a bench. Hands folded. Apron creased.

No cape. No hero pose. Just present.

For a moment, nobody moved.

Then someone stepped forward with a cup of coffee.

Plain. Black. No lid.

He set it carefully at Mara's feet and stepped back.

Another followed. Then another.

Soon, the tile in front of the bench held a crooked line of cups, steam rising like breath.

A voice from the back said it quietly. Serious this time.

"Mar-a."

Another voice answered.

"Mar-a."

More and more joined in, echoing off the walls.

Practice, not a chant. Not yet. Like they were testing the name in their mouths, making sure it belonged to a real person.

People who had taken coffee from her for years were now carrying it to her with both hands, careful not to spill. One man set a cup on the bench beside Mara's knee, like he was saving her a place.

Someone sniffed. Someone laughed once, too sharp, then stopped.

Maddy shifted at the back, tablet rising like reflex. Her eyes moved with the sound, counting mouths.

"Be mindful," she said, too crisp for a memorial.

"If this turns into a disruption, I'll file a complaint. Names are being recorded."

A few heads turned.

Nobody stopped.

Maddy's jaw tightened as if the room had violated policy by breathing wrong. She made a note anyway.

Eleanor waited.

When the room settled into something like quiet, she spoke without raising her voice.

"There's one more thing," she said.

Heads turned.

"The café has a new name," Eleanor continued.

She paused, then flicked a switch. The new sign lit up behind the garden glass:

Mara Flores Café.

People looked around, confused, like they expected the building to respond.

Eleanor reached into her pocket and pulled out a small metal tin.

She opened it with her thumb. The click was tiny, but it carried.

She took one mint and held it for a moment, then placed it gently between Mara's folded bronze hands.

No explanation.

A few people stared at the mint like they didn't know what they were seeing. Others looked away.

Janis approached last with a flat catering tray.

Seven black coffees. No lids.

She set the tray on the bench beside Mara.

One for her. Six for the ones who stayed behind.

She sat on the other side, shoulders squared, holding a place for someone who wasn't late, just gone.

"Good work," Janis said quietly.

"All of you."

***

Marcy, Sammy, and Janis all went back to the café.

The lobby noise fell off behind them like a door shutting. The café was dim, half-lit, the espresso machine sitting there like it was waiting to be told what to do.

The three looked back at the sign. It looked different.

New acrylic. Backlit. Clean.

Mara Flores Café.

They stood staring at it for a long time without moving.

"Yeah," Marcy said to the counter, to the grinder, to the empty space where Mara used to stand. "They finally got one thing right."

Sammy stood at attention, staring at the sign, and gave the two-finger salute, and instantly, Janis and Marcy followed.

Sammy and Janis walked toward the exit, leaving Marcy alone.

Marcy set up for close on muscle memory. Wiped the bar. Counted the tips. Stacked the cups. All the small rituals that kept the day from spilling.

Her hand drifted to the second towel again, the one she'd hidden. She pulled it out, stared at it, then set it beside the register anyway, right where Mara would have wanted it.

When she shut the machine down, the café went quiet enough that she could hear the building breathe.

Marcy flipped the lights off.

Dark.

Then she reached back and turned one light on over the counter. Just the work light. The one Mara always left on if she knew she'd be back in the morning.

Mara hated coming back to a dark café.

Marcy locked the gate, tested it twice, and stepped out into the lobby.

Through the glass, she could still see the garden bench. People were still there, sitting like they didn't know what came next. Coffee cups clustered at Mara's feet like offerings that had become habit in a single day.

Marcy didn't interrupt them.

She tightened her jacket, turned away, and went to the arcade.

THANK YOU

Thank you for reading *The Legend of Mara Flores*. I hope you enjoyed reading it as much as I enjoyed writing it. If you enjoyed this book, I would deeply appreciate it if you took a few minutes to write a review on Amazon.com (https://amzn.to/45RunAo). Even a short review would be fine. Reviews are vital to a book's success, and authors like myself enjoy reading what readers say.

Arthur M. Mills, Jr.

ABOUT THE AUTHOR

Arthur Mills served for more than two decades as an Army Intelligence Warrant Officer, specializing in piecing together what others missed: patterns, threats, enemy intent, and clandestine activity. He trained intelligence professionals, built threat models, and briefed commanders and world leaders on global threats and battlefield strategy. After retiring from the military, he moved into private investigation, focusing on missing persons, human trafficking, opposition research, and domestic terrorism. He holds a degree in Counter Terrorism Studies.

He has been writing books since 2006 and is an award-winning author. He publishes under his own name, though much of what he has written has appeared under pseudonyms. Readers may already know those titles without knowing they are his. The separation is intentional. His books invite readers to interpret what is hidden, and so does the way he publishes them.

VISIT ME ONLINE

- Website: www.branchingplotbooks.com

- Facebook: www.facebook.com/BranchingPlotBooks

- Goodreads: www.goodreads.com/artmills

- LinkedIn: www.linkedin.com/company/branching-plot-books

- YouTube: www.youtube.com/@branchingplotbooks8807

- Amazon Author's Profile: https://www.amazon.com/author/arthurmills